Mrs. Crowe's Christmas Ghosts

By Catherine Crowe

Edited by Karen Joan Kohoutek

Mrs. Crowe's Christmas Ghosts

This revised edition, introduction, & footnotes by Karen Joan Kohoutek, under the Creative Commons license Attribution-NonCommercial-ShareAlike.

Skull and Book Press 2018

ISBN: 978-0-578-21413-9

Originally published in 1859 as *Ghosts and Family Legends: A Volume for Christmas*, by "Mrs. Crowe, Authoress of 'Night Side of Nature,' &c.", by Thomas Cautley Newby (Welbeck Street, Cavendish Square, London), and printed by "Ostell, Printer; Hart Street, Bloomsbury."

The cover image is from Elliot Madge's *Original Christmas Stories, Etc.* (1883). There are no known copyright restrictions.

Contact us at octoberzine@gmail.com

About the Ghosts

This volume collects the stories originally published in *Ghosts and Family Legends: A Volume for Christmas* (1859), which author Catherine Crowe hoped would "prove a not uninteresting companion for a Christmas fireside" (from the original "Preface").

A follow-up to Crowe's hugely successful 1848 book *The Night Side of Nature* (frequently name-checked here), this work continues to preach open-minded on the subject of occult experience, which she believed should be judged and investigated like all other phenomena, rather than dismissed out of hand.

Crowe wrote popular novels and plays, but was best known for her nonfiction works on the supernatural. Translating some of her related ghost stories from the original German, she brought the word "poltergeist" into the English language. Born in England, she spent much of her career in Edinburgh, and her social circle included writers like Thomas de Quincey, Charles Dickens, and Hans Christian Andersen.

Her date of birth has been stated as both 1790 and 1803, and her death as both in 1872 and 1876.

About the Text

The text has been edited to the grammatical conventions of modern readers, in spelling, paragraph length, and punctuation, since, apparently, the Victorians couldn't get enough of the semi-colon. There was also some format-tweaking due to the numerous stories within stories, and dialogue inside dialogue, since much of the original took place within confusing double quotations.

In addition, I wound up focusing on the "Ghosts" section and jettisoning the "Family Legends," subtitled "Legends of the Earthbound," which made up the second part of the book. Fortunately, the original version can be viewed at various sites like the Internet Archive, Hathi Trust, and Project Gutenberg, and I hope you'll look them up.

The use of initials for names and places was the common practice at the time, to mark them as real people and locations without revealing any personal information. A few of the participants in the ghost story sessions have been identified in the footnotes.

For Further Research

Ayres, Brenda. *Silent Voices: Forgotten Novels by Victorian Women Writers*. Westport [CT]: Praeger, 2003.

Crowe, Catherine. *The Night Side of Nature: Or Ghosts and Ghost Seers*. Edited by Gillian Bennett. Ware: Wordsworth Editions, 2000.

Crowe, Catherine. *Spiritualism, and the Age We Live in*. New York: Cambridge University Press, 2011.

Heholt, Ruth. "Introduction." *The Story of Lilly Dawson*, by Catherine Crowe. Brighton: Victorian Secrets, 2015. 5 -16.

Preface

It happened that I spent the last winter in a large country mansion, in the north of England, where we had a succession of visitors, and all manner of amusements -- dancing, music, cards, billiards, and other games.

Towards the end of December, 1857, however, the gaiety of the house was temporarily interrupted by a serious misfortune that occurred to one of the party, which, in the evening, occasioned us to assemble with grave faces round the drawing-room fire, where we fell to discussing the slight tenure by which we hold whatever blessings we enjoy, and the sad uncertainty of human life, as it affects us in its most mournful aspect -- the lives of those we love.

From this theme, the conversation branched out into various speculations regarding the great mysteries of the here and hereafter; the reunion of friends, and the possible interests of them that have passed away in the well-being of those they have left behind, 'til it fell, naturally, into the relation of certain experiences which almost everybody has had, more or less, and which were adduced to fortify the arguments of those who regard the future as less disjoined from the present than it is considered to be by theologians generally.

In short, we began to tell ghost stories, and although some of the party professed an utter disbelief in apparitions, they proved to be as fertile as the believers in their contributions -- relating something that had happened to themselves or their friends, as having undoubtedly occurred, or to all appearance, occurred -- only, with the reservation, that it must certainly have been a dream.

The substance of these conversations fills the following pages, and I have told the stories as nearly as possible in the words of the original narrators. Of course, I am not permitted to give their names. Nobody chooses to confess, in print, that he, or anybody belonging to him, has seen a ghost, or believes that he has seen one. There is a sort of odium attached to the imputation, that scarcely anyone seems equal to encounter, and no wonder, when wise people listen to the avowal with such strange incredulity, and pronounce you at the best a superstitious fool, or a patient afflicted with spectral illusions.

Under these circumstances, whether I have ever seen a ghost, myself, I must decline confiding to the public, but I take almost as courageous a step in avowing my entire and continued belief in the fact that others do occasionally see these things, and I assert, that most of those who related the events contained in the ensuing pages of this work, confessed to me their absolute conviction that they or their friends had actually seen and heard what they said they did.

CATHERINE CROWE.

15th October, 1858.

Round the Fire
First Evening

"But there are no ghosts now," objected Mr. R.

"Quite the contrary," said I. "I have no doubt there is nobody in this circle who has not either had some experience of the sort in his own person, or been made a confidant of such experiences by friends whose word on any other subject he would feel it impossible to doubt."

After some discussion on the existence of ghosts and cognate subjects, it was agreed that each should relate a story, restricting himself to circumstances that had either happened to himself or had been told him by somebody fully entitled to confidence, who had undergone the experience.

We followed the order in which we were sitting, and Miss P. began as follows:

I was some years ago engaged to be married to an officer in the --- regiment. Circumstances connected with our families prevented the union taking place as early as we had expected, and in the meanwhile Captain S., whose regiment was in the West Indies, was ordered to join. I need not say that this separation distressed us a good deal, but we consoled each other as well as we could by maintaining a constant correspondence, though there were no steam packets in those days, and letters were much longer on their way and less certain in their arrival than they are now. Still I heard pretty regularly, and had no reason for the least uneasiness.

One day that I had been out shopping, and had returned rather tired, I told my mother that I should go and lie down for an hour, for we were going out in the evening, and I was afraid I might have a headache, to which I am rather subject. So I went up to my room, took down a book and threw myself on the bed to read or sleep as it might happen. I had read a page or two, and feeling drowsy, had laid down the volume in order to compose myself to sleep, when I was aroused by a knock at my chamber door.

"Come in," I said, without turning my head, for I thought it was the maid, come to fetch the dress I was going to wear in the evening.

I heard the door open and a person enter, but the foot was not hers, and then I looked round and saw that it was Captain S. What came over me then I can't tell you. I knew little of mesmerism at that period, but I have since thought that when a spirit appears, it must have some power of mesmerizing the spectator, for I have heard other people who had been in similar situations describe very much what I experienced myself. I was perfectly calm, not in the least frightened or surprised, but transfixed. Of course, had I remained in my normal state, I should either have been amazed at seeing Captain S. so unexpectedly, especially in my chamber, or if I believed it an apparition, I should have been dreadfully distressed and alarmed. But I was neither, and I can't say whether I thought it himself or his ghost. I was passive, and my mind accepted the phenomenon without question of how such a thing could be.

Captain S. approached the bedside, and spoke to me exactly as he was in the habit of doing, and I answered him in the same manner. After the first greeting, he crossed the room to fetch a chair that stood by the dressing table. He wore his uniform, and when his back was turned, I remember distinctly seeing the seams of his coat behind. He brought the chair, and having seated himself by the bedside, he conversed with me for about half an hour. He then rose and, looking at his watch, said his time had expired and he must go. He bade me goodbye, and went out by the same door he had entered at.

The moment it closed on him, I knew what had happened. If my hypothesis be correct, his power over me ceased when he disappeared and I returned to my normal state. I screamed, and seized the bell rope which I rang with such violence that I broke it. My mother, who was in the room underneath, rushed upstairs, followed by the servants. They found me on the floor in a fainting state, and for some time I was unable to communicate the cause of my agitation.

At length, being somewhat calmed, I desired the servants might leave the room, and then I told my mother what had happened. Of course, she thought it was a dream. In vain I assured her it was not, and pointed to the chair which, wonderful to say, had been actually brought to the bedside by the spirit -- there it stood exactly as it had been placed by him; luckily nobody had moved it.

I said, "You know where that chair usually stands. When you were up here a little while ago it was in its usual place -- so it was when I lay down -- I never moved it; it was placed there by Captain S."

My mother was greatly perplexed. She found me so confident and clear, yet, the thing appeared to her impossible.

From that time, I only thought of Captain S. as one departed from this life; suspense and its agonies were spared me. I was certain. Accordingly, about a month afterwards, when one morning Major B. of the --- regiment sent in his card, I said to my mother, "Now you'll see; he comes to tell me of Henry's death."

It was so. Captain S. had died of fever on the day he paid me that mysterious visit.

We asked Miss P. if any similar circumstance had ever occurred to her before or since.

"Never," she answered. "I never saw anything of the sort but on that occasion."

"I have no experience of my own to relate," said Dr. W:

But in the course of my late tour in Scotland, I went amongst other places to Skye,[1] and I found the whole island talking of an event that had just happened there, which may perhaps interest you. There was a tradesman in Portree[2] of the name of Robertson; I believe he was a sort of general dealer, as shopkeepers frequently are in those remote localities. Whatever his business was, however, it frequently took him to the other islands or the mainland to make purchases. He had arranged to go on one of these expeditious, I think to Raasa,[3] when a friend called to inform him that a meeting of the inhabitants was to be held on some public question in which he, Robertson, was much interested.

"You had better defer going 'til after Friday," said Mr. Brown. "We can't do without you, and it's very possible you may not get back in time."

"Oh, yes, I can do all my business, and be back very well on Thursday," said Mr. Robertson, objecting that if he waited over Friday it would be no use going 'til Monday. Brown tried to persuade him to alter his plans, but in vain.

"However," said he, "you may rely on seeing me on Thursday, if you'll look in, in the evening; as I would not miss the meeting on any account."

This conversation took place at an early hour on Tuesday morning. Immediately afterwards Mr. Robertson bade his wife and children good-bye, and proceeded to the boat which left at eleven o'clock, having on board, besides himself, two other passengers, and two boatmen.

On Thursday evening, Mr. Brown, who had been busying himself in fortifying and encouraging their adherents against the next day, and had taken upon himself to answer for his friend Robertson's presence, as soon as he had finished business, set off to keep his appointment with the latter, anxious to ascertain that he was arrived.

His anxiety was soon relieved, for on his way he met him.

---

[1] An island in the Highlands of Scotland.
[2] The capital of the Isle of Skye, founded as a fishing village in the 18th century.
[3] An island, also known as Raasay, between the Isle of Skye and the Scottish mainland.

"Well, here you are," said he, holding out his hand.

"Yes," answered Robertson, not appearing to notice the hand. "I have kept my promise."

Upon that Mr. Brown introduced the subject of the meeting, and mentioned the hopes he had of carrying the question, with which Robertson seemed satisfied, but as soon as possible turning the conversation into another direction, he began talking to his friend about his wife and children, and certain arrangements he had wished to be made respecting his property.

His mind seemed so much more engrossed with these matters than the meeting, that little was said upon the latter subject, and Mr. Brown, having parted with him in the street, rather wondered why he chose such a moment to discuss his private affairs.

The next morning, at the appointed hour, the principal inhabitants of the place assembled in a public room at the Tun.[4] Brown, who wanted to say a word to Robertson, lingered at the door, but as he did not come, he thought he must have arrived before himself, and went upstairs.

"Is Robertson here?" said he, on entering the room.

"No,' said one. "I'm afraid he's not come back from Raasa."

"Oh, yes," said Brown. "He'll be here; I saw him yesterday evening."

They then discoursed about the matter in hand for some time, 'til finding the chairman was about to proceed to business, Robertson's absence was again reverted to.

"I know he's come back," said one, "for I saw him standing at his own door as I passed last night."

"He can't have forgotten it," said another.

"Certainly not, for we spoke of it last night," said Brown.

"Perhaps he's ill," suggested somebody.

"Just send your man to Mr. Robertson's, and say we are waiting for him," said Brown to the landlord.

The landlord left the room to do so, and, in the meantime, they proceeded to business.

Presently, the landlord re-entered the room, saying that Mrs. Robertson answered that her husband had not returned from Raasa, and that she did not much expect he would be back until night.

"Nonsense," cried Brown. "Why, I saw the man yesterday according to appointment, and had a long conversation with him."

---

[4] A "large cask" or keg of beer. The word is found in the name of various pubs.

"I am sure he's come back," said one who had spoke before. "I was coming down the street on the other side of the way, and I saw him standing at the door with his apron on. I should have crossed over to speak to him, but I was in a hurry."

"It's extraordinary," said the landlord. "Mrs. Robertson declares he's not come."

Some jokes were then passed about the apparent defection of Robertson from his spouse, and the meeting concluded their business without him, his party being exceedingly annoyed at his absence, which they thought not fair to the cause.

"He should have given us his support."

"I suppose he has altered his opinions."

"Then he had better have said so."

"It struck me, certainly, that he was rather lukewarm on the subject when I talked to him last night, but on Tuesday I saw him just before he started, and he said he would not miss the meeting on any account. I'll go and look after him and know what he means."

Accordingly, Brown proceeded to his friend's house, and found Mrs. Robertson and her children at dinner.

"Weel, Mr. Brown," she said. "So your meeting's over."

"Aye," said he. "But where's Robertson? Why didn't he keep his word with us?"

"Why, you see, I dare say he meant to be back. Indeed, I know he did. But business won't be neglected, and I suppose he could not manage it."

"Do you mean to say he's not come back?" said Brown.

"Sure, I do," answered Mrs. R. "Of course, he'd have been at the meeting if he had."

"But people saw him last night, standing at his own door," answered the cautious Brown.

"Na, na, Mr. Brown, don't you believe that," said Mrs. R., laughing. "They that say that had too much whiskey in their een."[5]

The children laughed at the idea of anybody seeing their father when he was at Raasa, and on the whole it was evident, that if John Robertson had returned, it was unknown to his family. But what could be his reason for so strange a proceeding, and why, if he wanted to evade the meeting, had he needlessly shown himself at all? Why not really stay away from Portree?

However, Robertson did not appear, and later in the day the landlord of the Tun said to Brown, as he was passing the door, "You

---

[5] Scots slang for "eyes."

must have been mistaken about seeing Mr. Robertson; the boat from Raasa is not come in."

"Then he must have come over by some other, for I not only saw him but walked and talked with him. I can't think what he can mean by playing at Hide and Seek in this way."

"It's very extraordinary," said the landlord, "for I am expecting a hamper from Raasa, and so, hearing from you that Mr. Robertson was come, I went down to inquire about it, but they declare no boat of any sort has come in these two days. The wind's right against them."

"I know the boat from Raasa is not come back," said the porter, "for I saw Jenny McGill just now, and she says her husband is not returned."

"Really you'll persuade me that I'm not in my right senses," said the perplexed Brown. "If ever I saw Robertson in my life I saw him last night. I was going to call upon him, as he had asked me to do so before he went away, but I met him, not far from my own house, and what is more, he told me of a thing I did not know before, regarding a purchase he had made, and spoke of what he intended to do with it."

"It's most extraordinary," said the landlord.

"Eh, sirs," said an old fishwife, who was standing by, "I wish it may not be John Robertson's ghaist[6] that ye saw, for the wind's sair agin[7] them, and I'd a bad dream about Jamie McGill last night."

They all laughed, but this was the first suggestion of the sort that had been made, and though he would not confess it, Brown began to feel rather uncomfortable, the more so as several things were recalled to his memory that had not struck him at the time.

He remembered that Robertson had avoided shaking hands with him, either on meeting or parting, as was his wont. He had even then been struck with the grave tone of his conversation, and with his choosing that particular moment for pressing on his friend's attention what did not appear to have any urgent interest at present.

Then it occurred to him that he looked ill and sad. He had attributed this to fatigue, but now, putting everything together, he could not help feeling a considerable degree of uneasiness. He kept hovering about Robertson's house, and from that to the shore all day; went to bed at night quite nervous; and by the next afternoon the alarm had spread and become universal. It was not without cause.

John Robertson never came back. The boat had been lost -- how, was not known, as all on board had perished. However, Mr. Brown

---

[6] Scots word for "ghost."
[7] Scots for "hard against."

took upon himself to be the friend and guardian of the bereaved family, and the information he received in that melancholy interview he was enabled to turn much to the advantage of their circumstances.

"A very remarkable story," said I.

"Yes," answered Dr. W. "Very remarkable indeed, if true."

"And is it not true?" I said. "Remember, we are upon honor. I should think it a very ill compliment if any one attempted to mystify us with an invented story."

"I did not invent it, I assure you," replied Dr. W. "I give it you as it was given to me on the spot. If you ask me if I believe it, I can't say I do."

"Do you think the people who told you believed it?"

"They certainly appeared to do so."

"And did it seem generally believed?"

"I can't say but it did, but of course, one must have wonderfully strong evidence before one could believe such a thing as that."

"Granted; but unless you had seen the thing yourself, you cannot have stronger evidence of a phenomenon of that description, than that it was believed by those who had good reason to know the grounds of their belief. They were able to judge how far Mr. Brown was worthy of credit, and they had the advantage of having witnessed his demeanor at the public meeting, when he asserted that he had walked and talked with Robertson, at a time he could not possibly know if he was telling a lie, that the man would not sooner or later return to confute him.

"Besides, as far as we see, it would have been a useless and wicked lie, inasmuch as it was calculated to make the man's family very uneasy. His subsequent conduct does not at all countenance the persuasion that he was capable of such a proceeding."

"Certainly not, but you know the Scotch are very superstitious."

"I can't agree with you. The higher and lower classes of the towns are exactly similar in that respect to the same classes of England. In all countries the lower classes are more disposed to put faith in these things, because they believe in their traditions and adhere to the axiom that seeing is believing. The higher classes, on the other hand, are carefully educated not to believe in such traditions and to reject the axiom that seeing is believing, if the thing seen is a ghost. Now I freely admit, that our senses often deceive us, and that we think we see what we do not. Everybody with the slightest intelligence has, I suppose, learnt to distrust his own senses to a certain extent. But why on one particular point we should reject their evidence altogether, I never could understand."

"You have heard, I suppose of spectral illusions?" said the Doctor.

"Of course I have, and admit their existence, but we have so many cases on our side, that doctrine will not cover, and it is so impossible for you to prove that any particular case of ghost-seeing falls under that head, that it is no use discussing the subject. It complicates the difficulty I confess, but can never decide the question. I was going to say, however, that the shopkeepers and middle classes of Scotland are anything but what you mean by superstitious. The class to whom Brown and Robertson belong is the most hardheaded, argumentative, and matter of fact in the kingdom, and their religion, which is eminently unimaginative, so far from inducing a belief in ghosts, would have a precisely opposite tendency, because ghosts do not form an article of belief in either the longer or shorter catechism. In the remoter districts of the Highlands, the people are said to have more of what you would call superstition, but the same peculiarity is remarked in all mountainous regions, and as it has never been satisfactorily accounted for, we will not enter into the discussion now."

Round the Fire
Second Evening

"After the doctor's story, I fear mine will appear too trifling," said Mrs. M. "But as it is the only circumstance of the kind that ever happened to myself, I prefer giving it you to any of the many stories I have heard:

About fifteen years ago, I was staying with some friends at a magnificent old seat in Yorkshire, and our host being very much crippled with the gout, was in the habit of driving about the park and neighborhood in a low pony phaeton,[8] on which occasions, I often accompanied him. One of our favorite excursions was to the ruins of an old abbey just beyond the park, and we generally returned by a remarkably pretty rural lane leading to the village, or rather, small town of C.

One fine summer's evening we had just entered this lane, when seeing the hedges full of wild flowers, I asked my friend to let me alight and gather some. I walked on before the carriage picking honeysuckles and roses as I went along, 'til I came to a gate that led into a field. It was a common country gate, with a post on each side, and on one of these posts sat a large white cat, the finest animal of the kind I had ever seen. As I have a weakness for cats, I stopped to admire this sleek, fat puss, looking so wonderfully comfortable in a very uncomfortable position, the top of the post on which it was sitting, with its feet doubled up under it, being out of all proportion to its body, for no Angola ever rivaled it in size.

"Come on, gently," I called to my friend, "here's such a magnificent cat!" For I feared the approach of the phaeton would startle it away before he had seen it.

"Where?" said he, pulling up his horse opposite the gate.

"There," said I, pointing to the post. "Isn't it a beauty? I wonder if it would let me stroke it!"

"I see no cat," said he.

"There on the post," said I, but he declared he saw nothing, though puss sat there in perfect composure during this colloquy.

"Don't you see the cat, James?" said I, in great perplexity, to the groom.

"Yes, ma'am, a large white cat on that post."

---

[8] A small open carriage, pulled by one or two horses, that has noticeably large wheels.

I thought my friend must be joking, or else losing his eyesight, and I approached the cat, intending to take it in my arms, and carry it to the carriage, but as I drew near, she jumped off the post. Which was natural enough -- but to my surprise she jumped into nothing -- as she jumped she disappeared! No cat in the field -- none in the lane -- none in the ditch!

"Where did she go, James?"

"I don't know, ma'am, I can't see her," said the groom, standing up in his seat, and looking all round.

I was quite bewildered, but still I had no glimmering of the truth, and when I got into the carriage again, my friend said he thought I and James were dreaming, and I retorted that I thought he must be going blind.

I had a commission to execute as we passed through the town, and I alighted for that purpose at the little haberdasher's, and while they were serving me, I mentioned that I had seen a remarkably beautiful cat sitting on a gate in the lane, and asked if they could tell me who it belonged to, adding, it was the largest cat I ever saw.

The owners of the shop, and two women who were making purchases, suspended their proceedings, looked at each other, and then looked at me, evidently very much surprised.

"Was it a white cat, ma'am?" said the mistress.

"Yes, a white cat, a beautiful creature and --"

"Bless me!" cried two or three. "The lady's seen the White Cat of C. It hasn't been seen these twenty years."

"Master wishes to know if you'll soon be done, ma'am? The pony is getting restless," said James.

Of course, I hurried out, and got into the carriage, telling my friend that the cat was well known to the people at C., and that it was twenty years old.

In those days, I believe, I never thought of ghosts, and least of all should I have thought of the ghost of a cat, but two evenings afterwards, as we were driving down the lane, I again saw the cat in the same position, and again my companion could not see it, though the groom did. I alighted immediately, and went up to it.

As I approached, it turned its head, and looked full towards me with its soft, mild eyes, and a kindly expression, like that of a loving dog, and then, without moving from the post, it began to fade gradually away, as if it were a vapor, 'til it had quite disappeared. All this the groom saw as well as myself, and now there could be no mistake as to what it was.

A third time, I saw it in broad daylight, and my curiosity greatly awakened, I resolved to make further inquiries amongst the inhabitants of C., but before I had an opportunity of doing so, I was summoned away by the death of my eldest child, and I have never been in that part of the world since. However, I once mentioned the circumstance to a lady who was acquainted with that neighborhood, and she said she had heard of the White Cat of C., but had never seen it.

But as you may not think this story very interesting since it only relates to a cat, I will, if you please, tell you another, in which I was concerned, although I saw nothing myself.

"We shall be very happy," I said, "but I am far from thinking your story wanting in interest; in fact, to me it has a very peculiar interest. There are few friends so sincere as the animals who have loved us, and none that I, for my part, more earnestly desire to see again. I have had two dogs, in my life, who contributed much to my happiness while they lived, and never caused me a sorrow 'til they died. Besides, there is a deep mystery in the being of these creatures, which proud man never seeks to unravel, or condescends to speculate on.

"What is their relation to the human race? Why are these spiritual germs embodied in those forms and made subject to man, that hard and cruel master? Who assumes to be their superior, because he is endowed with some higher faculties, the most of which he grossly misuses. How beautiful are their characters when studied! How wonderful their intelligence when cultivated! How willing they are to serve us when kindly treated! But man, by his cruelty, ignorance, laziness, and want of judgment, spoils their temper, blunts their intelligence, deteriorates their nature, and then punishes them for being what he himself has made them. Well might Chalmers exclaim, 'All nature groans beneath the cruelty of man.'[9] Why are these creatures, sinless, as far as we see, placed here as the subjects of this barbarous, unthinking tyrant? That has always appeared to me a solemn question."

After this little digression, Mrs. M. continued as follows:

---

[9] Likely Thomas Chalmers (1780 -1847), a Scottish minister of the Free Church of Scotland, and writer on natural theology. The quote is probably a paraphrase of his ideas as stated in *On the Adaptation of External Nature to the Moral and Intellectual Constitution of Man, Vol. 1*. In speaking of the relationship between man and the "inferior animals," Chalmers says "the men who use them as instruments of service often discharge the most outrageous wrath upon them – acting the part of ferocious tyrants towards these wretched victims of their cruelty."

I had been travelling on the continent, and was staying at Brussels on my way home. The bedroom I occupied was within another, in which slept my faithful maid, Rachel, and one of my children. I had been in bed sometime, and had not been to sleep, when I heard Rachel's voice, saying something which I did not distinctly hear, and before I could ask what it was, she uttered a cry that immediately brought me to her bedside.

I found her in a state of violent agitation, and as soon as she was composed enough to speak, she told me that she had not been long in bed when she heard a voice call her, which she supposed to be mine, and immediately afterwards, in the glass which was opposite the foot of the bed, she saw a figure in white enter and proceed to the other end of the room.

She concluded it was me in my night dress, and that I had only mentioned her name to ascertain if she was awake. Fearing to disturb the child, who was restless, she lay still, and did not answer. The figure went back through the door, but presently returned again, and seemed to be looking about for something, whereupon she half sat up in bed. When it approached, and laid its hand heavily on her knee, there was something painful in the pressure, and she exclaimed, "Oh, don't do that, ma'am!" but she had scarcely uttered the words when she discerned the features, and saw it was her sister.

The phantom looked sadly at her, and then retreating to the opposite corner, disappeared. This circumstance, in spite of my arguments and suggestions that it was a dream, made a very painful impression on her. She felt sure some misfortune had happened, and so it proved. Her sister had died on that night, leaving a family of young children, about whom, in her last moments, she was very anxious.

"Cases of that sort are very numerous," said Lady A. "I know of two which I can give upon perfectly good authority:

A friend of mine was sitting a few years since in the drawing room at her country seat. There was a door at each end, leading to other rooms, both of which were open. A slight rustle caused her to raise her eyes from her work, when she saw her nephew enter at one door, walk straight through, and out at the other. The young man was at college, and she had no reason to expect him then, but concluding some unforeseen business had brought him, and that he was in search of her, she called, "Arthur, here I am," and pursued him into the adjoining room, and then into the hall.

Receiving no answer, and not being able to find him in any direction, she rang for the servants, and inquired where he was, but they did not know. They had seen nothing of him. She insisted he had arrived, and he was sought for all over the house and grounds in vain. The thing remained perfectly incomprehensible, 'til the post brought a letter, announcing that the young man had been drowned on that day.

Another instance, equally well established, is that of Dr. C., of Dublin. He resided with his family some few miles from the city, I believe, at or near Howth,[10] and when he returned in the evening after visiting his patients, he frequently, to save time, took a short cut across some sands, which in certain states of the tide were not always safe.

Mrs. C. had often entreated him to relinquish this practice, and take the more circuitous way, but he thought he was too well acquainted with the place to run any danger. One evening that they were expecting him, as usual, to dinner, his brother, who was standing at the window, saw him arrive. He rode a white horse, and was therefore a conspicuous object. When the dinner hour came, as he had not appeared in the drawing room, his brother and Mrs. C., to whom the latter had mentioned having seen him, desired the servants to seek him in his dressing room, and ask if he was ready.

He was not in his room, nor was he anywhere to be found. Neither had any of the servants seen him, nor was his horse in the stable. Mr. C., however, confident of his arrival, suggested that he might be gone to visit some sick person in the neighborhood, so they waited. But in vain; news presently arrived that horse and man had been drowned that evening in crossing the sands.

There was scarcely anyone present unacquainted with examples of this kind of appearance amongst their family or friends, but Captain L. related to us a case still more curious and unaccountable that had happened to himself in India, when he was in the Himalayas:

I was just finishing my breakfast one morning, when my servant entered and announced a visitor. It was Captain P. B. of ours, who came to invite me to a game of billiards. Our billiard-room was situated about a mile beyond my quarter, and Captain B., who lived at the other extremity, had to pass my residence to go to it.

"Are you going up there now?" I said.

"Yes," said he. "Will you come?"

---

[10] A village near Dublin.

"Why, I can't come directly," I answered, "for I have a letter to write first, but if you'll go on, I'll join you presently."

He left me, and as soon as I had written my letter, I started for the billiard-room. When I entered it, Captain P. B. was not there, nor, indeed, anybody but the marker, which was not surprising, as it was earlier than we usually went there.

"Where's Captain B?" I said.

"Don't know, sir; he has not been here yet."

"Not been here?"

"No, sir, not today."

Thinking, that as I was not ready, he had filled up the interval by going somewhere else, I began knocking about the balls, every now and then looking out of the window, expecting to see him approach, but when this had lasted upwards of two hours, I began to be rather impatient, and was just thinking of going away, when I saw him approaching with his wife in an open carriage from an opposite direction.

"A pretty fellow you are, to keep me kicking my heels here waiting for you," said I, as he entered the room.

"Keep you waiting!" he said. "I have not kept you waiting."

"Why, I've been here these two hours and more."

"How was I to know that? I did not know you were coming up here."

"Why, I told you I'd come as soon as I had finished my letter."

"My dear fellow, what are you talking about?" exclaimed my friend, in evident surprise. "When did you tell me so? I don't recollect making any appointment to meet you today."

"What! Not this morning, as you were passing my quarter?" said I, amazed in my turn. "Didn't you ask me to come and play a game at billiards, and didn't I tell you I'd come as soon as I had finished my letter? And I did."

P. B. looked at me as if he thought I'd suddenly become insane, but as I suppose my countenance did not confirm that impression, he said, "Here's some mistake. When do you suppose I made this appointment with you?"

"Suppose!" I answered, rather indignant. "What do you mean by suppose? Didn't you come into my quarter about three hours ago, just as I was finishing breakfast, and ask me to come up here and play a game at billiards with you?"

"No, it must have been somebody else. Who gave you the message?"

"Message! There was no message," I answered, quite bewildered. "You came in yourself. You know you did. What's the use of trying to hoax one?"

"I don't know whether you are trying to hoax *me*," replied P. B. "But upon my soul I have not been in your quarter today, nor have I seen you at all, 'til I entered this room. Moreover, I went with my wife at an early hour to breakfast with Captain D., and we are now returning thence, and I told the coachman to set me down here as he passed."

This was most confounding, and as we were both equally positive in what we asserted, we left the billiard-room together, and proceeded to take the testimony of my servant. On being asked who he had introduced when I was finishing breakfast, he unhesitatingly answered, "Captain B." His account, in short, coincided entirely with mine.

"Now then," said Captain B. "As you have your witness, you must hear mine," and we went on to his quarter, where I received the most satisfactory and unimpeachable evidence, that what he said was correct. He had left home with Mrs. B. at six o'clock, and gone by appointment to breakfast with Captain D., who lived quite in a different direction to my quarter, and Captain D. afterwards testified to his never having left his house 'til he stepped into the carriage with his wife.

This event created a great sensation at the time, and people endeavored by every means to explain it away, but nobody ever could. Captain B. did not like it at all, and his wife and family were very much alarmed, but nothing ensued, and I believe he is alive and well at this moment.

We next turned to Madame Von B., who said she knew so many cases of spiritual appearances, and occurrences of that nature, that she was rather perplexed by the abundance of her recollections. Amongst these she selected the following on account of its singularity:

We resided a great deal on the continent before I was married, and my mother had a favorite maid, called Françoise, who lived with her many years: a most trustworthy, excellent creature, in whom she had the greatest confidence, insomuch, that when I married, being very young and very inexperienced, as she was obliged to separate from me herself, she transferred Françoise to my service, considering her better able to take care of me than anybody else.

I was living in Paris then, where Françoise, who was a native of Metz,[11] had some relations settled in business, whom she often used to

---

[11] A French city in the Lorraine region.

visit. She was generally very chatty when she returned from these people, for I knew all her affairs, and through her, all their affairs, and I took an interest in whatever concerned her or hers.

One Sunday evening, after she had been spending the afternoon with this family, observing that she was unusually silent, I said to her, while she was undressing me, "Well, Françoise, haven't you anything to tell me? How are your friends? Has Madame Pelletier got rid of her *grippe?*"[12]

Françoise started as if I had awakened her out of a reverie, and said, "Oh! *oui, Madame; oui, mercé; elle se porte bien aujourd'hui.*"[13]

"And Monsieur Pelletier and the children, are they well?"

"*Oui, Madame, merci; ils se portent bien.*"[14]

These curt answers were so unlike those she generally gave me, that I was sure her mind was preoccupied, and that something had happened since we parted in the morning, so I turned round to look her in the face, saying, "*Mais, qu'avez vous donc, Françoise? Qu'est ce qu'il y a?*"[15]

Then I saw what I had not observed before, that she was very pale, and that her cheeks had a glazed look, which showed that she had been crying.

"*Mais, ma bonne Françoise,*" I said. "*Vous avez quelque chose -- est il arrivé quelque malheur à Metz?*"[16]

"*C'est cela,*[17] Madame," answered Françoise, who had a brother there whom she had not seen for several years, but to whom she still continued affectionately attached. His name was Benoît, and he was in a good service as *garde forestier*[18] to a nobleman who possessed very extensive estates, *près de chez nous,*[19] as Françoise said.

He had a wife and children, and some time before the period I am referring to, Françoise had told me, with great satisfaction, that in order to make him more comfortable, the Prince de M--- had given Benoît the privilege of gathering up all the dead wood in the forest to sell for firewood, which, as the estate was very large, rendered his situation extremely profitable. When she said "*c'est cela,* Madame," Françoise, who had just encased me in my dressing gown, sunk into a chair, and

---

[12] Influenza.

[13] "Yes, thank you, Madame. She is doing well today."

[14] "Yes, Madame, thank you. They are very well."

[15] "But what about you, Françoise? What's the matter?"

[16] "But my dear Françoise, there is something. Has anything unfortunate happened at Metz?"

[17] "That's it."

[18] A forest ranger.

[19] Near our house.

having declared that she was "*bête, très bête*,"[20] she gave way to a hearty good cry, after which, being somewhat relieved, she told me the following strange story.

"You remember," she said, "that the prince was so good as to give Benoît all the dead wood of the forest -- and a great thing it was for him and his family, as you will think, when I tell you it was worth upwards of two thousand francs a year to him. In short, he was growing rich, and perhaps he was getting to think too much of his money and too little of the *bon Dieu*[21] -- at all events, this privilege which the prince gave him to make him comfortable, and which made him a great man amongst the foresters, has been the cause of a dreadful calamity."

"How?" said I.

"We never heard anything of what had happened," said she, "until yesterday, when Monsieur Pelletier received a letter from Benoît's wife, and another from a cousin of ours, relating what I am going to tell you, and saying that both he and his family had wished to keep it secret, but that was no longer possible."

'Well, and what has happened?"

"*La chose la plus incroyable! Eh bien*, Madame,[22] it appears that one day last autumn, Benoît went out in the forest to gather the dead wood. He had his cart with him, and as he gathered it he bound it into faggots[23] and threw it in the cart. He had extended his search this day to a remote part of the forest, and found himself in a spot he did not remember to have visited before. Indeed, it was evident to him that he had not, or he could not have escaped seeing an old wooden cross which was lying on the ground, and had apparently fallen into that recumbent position from old age.

"It was such a cross as is usually set up where a life has been lost, whether by murder or suicide, or sometimes when poor wanderers are frozen to death or lost in the deep winter snows. He looked about for the grave, but saw no indication of one, and he tried to remember if any catastrophe had happened there in his time, but could recall none. He took up the cross and examined it. He saw that the wood was decayed, and it bore such marks of antiquity, that he had no doubt the person whose grave it had marked had died before he was born. It looked as if it might be a hundred years old.

"*Eh bien*," said Françoise, wiping her eyes, into which the tears kept starting. "Of course you will think that Benoît, or anybody in the

---

[20] "Stupid, very stupid!"

[21] The Good Lord.

[22] "The most incredible thing! Well, Madame ..."

[23] A bundle of twigs used for firewood.

world who had the fear of God before his eyes, as he could not find the grave to replace it as it should be, would have laid it reverently down where he had found it, saying a prayer for the soul of the deceased. But, alas! The demon of avarice tempted him, and he had not the heart to forego that poor cross, but bound it up into a faggot with the rest of the dead wood he found there, and threw it into his cart!"

"Well, Françoise," said I. "You know I am not a Catholic, but I respect the custom of erecting these crosses, and I do think your brother was very wrong. I suppose he has lost the prince's favour by such impious greediness."

"*Pire que ça!*"[24] she replied. "It appears that while he was committing this wicked action, he felt an extraordinary chill come over him, which made him think that, though it had been a mild day, the evening must have suddenly turned very cold, and hastily throwing the faggot into his cart, he directed his steps homeward. But walk as he would, he still felt this chill down his back, so that he turned his head to look where the wind blew from, when he saw, with some dismay, a mysterious-looking figure following close upon his footsteps. It moved noiselessly on, and was covered with a sort of black mantle that prevented his discerning the features.

"Not liking its appearance, he jumped into the cart and drove home as fast as he could, without looking behind him, and when he got into his own farmyard he felt quite relieved, particularly as when he alighted he saw no more of this unpleasant-looking stranger. So he began unloading his cart, taking out the faggots, one by one, and throwing them upon the ground, but when he threw down the one that contained the cross, he received a blow upon his face, so sharp that it made him stagger and involuntarily shout aloud.

"His wife and children were close by, but there was no one else to be seen, and they would have disbelieved him and fancied he had accidentally hit himself with the faggot, but that they saw the distinct mark on his cheek of a blow given with an open hand. However, he went into supper perplexed and uncomfortable, but when he went to bed this fearful phantom stood by his side, silent and terrible, visible to him, but invisible to others. In short, Madame, this awful figure haunted him 'til, in spite of his shame, he resolved to consult our cousin Jerome about it.

"But Jerome laughed, and said it was all fancy and superstition. 'You got frightened at having brought away this poor devil's cross, and then you fancy he's haunting you,' said he.

---

[24] "Worse than that!"

"But Benoît declared that he had thought nothing about the cross, except that it would make firewood, and that he had no more believed in ghosts than Jerome. 'But now,' said he, 'Something must be done. I can get no sleep and am losing my health; if you can't help me, I must go to the priest and consult him.'

"'Why don't you take back the cross and put it where you found it?' said Jerome.

"'Because I am afraid to touch it and dare not go to that part of the forest.'

"So Jerome, who did not believe a word about the ghost, offered to go with him and replace the cross. Benoît gladly accepted, more especially, as he said he saw the apparition standing even then beside him, apparently listening to the conversation. Jerome laughed at the idea; however, Benoît lifted the cross reverently into the cart and away they went into the forest. When they reached the spot, Benoît pointed out the tree under which he had found it, and as he was shaking and trembling, Jerome took up the cross and laid it on the ground, but as he did so he received a violent blow from an invisible hand, and at the same moment saw Benoît fall to the ground.

"He thought he had been struck too, but it afterwards appeared that he had fainted from having seen the phantom with its upraised hand striking his cousin. However, they left the cross and came away, but there was an end to Jerome's laughter, and he was afraid the apparition would now haunt him. Nothing of the sort happened, but poor Benoît's health has been so shaken by this frightful occurrence that he cannot get the better of it. His friends have advised change of scene, and he is coming to Paris next week."

This was the story Françoise told me, and in a few days I heard he had arrived and was staying with Monsieur Pelletier, but the shock had been too great for his nerves, and he died shortly after. They assured me that previous to that fatal expedition into the forest, he had been a hale, hearty man, totally exempt from superstitious fancies of any sort, and in short, wholly devoted to advancing his worldly prosperity and getting money.

Round the Fire
Third Evening

"I don't know that I could tell you anything interesting in the way of ghost stories. I have never attended to them, though I have heard a great many," said Colonel C. "But I can tell you an extraordinary circumstance which may, perhaps, be considered of a spiritual nature, and which I can myself vouch for the truth of:

My father, when I was young, resided in the South of England. I shall not give the name of the place, nor of the people immediately concerned, if these stories are to be published, because, for anything I know, some persons may survive to whom the publication might give pain. I lived there with him and my mother and sisters. Our house was on the road between two large towns, situated about eight miles distant from each other, and though we had a little ground and a short avenue in front, we were not more than half a quarter of a mile from the highway.

When all was still, we could distinctly hear the carts and carriages as they passed, and even distinguish by the sound of the wheels what kind of vehicle it was. There was a carrier that plied between these two towns, whom I will call Healy, and as everything we used we had from B., he was generally at our house three or four times a week. In short, he did our marketing, in a great degree, my mother giving him an order, as he passed, for what he was to bring back, and many a time Healy has smuggled a novel from the circulating library for my sisters, or done little commissions for me that I could not so well manage for myself.

All this made him a popular character with us, for he was very obliging, but for all that, he did not bear the best of characters. It was his interest to be well with us, and the gentry in general, who were his customers, and he understood that too well to incur our ill-will, but by his equals and inferiors he was looked upon with a less favorable eye.

They had nothing very positive to allege against him, but they thought him a hard, griping, greedy man, who was honest in his dealings with us because the slightest suspicion would have ruined his trade, but who would take an advantage when he thought no possible damage to himself could accrue from it. He was about forty years of age, tall, with a long face, prominent nose, and dark complexion. His shoulders were round, but his frame was wiry, and he was reputed very strong.

One evening, between thirty and forty years ago, towards the beginning of winter, we were expecting Healy. My mother was solicitous about some provisions she had ordered for an approaching dinner-party, and I was very anxious for the arrival of a cricket bat that I wanted for use the day after the next. Of course, long before the time he usually arrived, I was looking out for him, and fancying him late, I said, "I wondered Healy was not come!"

Upon which my father looked at his watch, and found that it wanted full half an hour of his time, which was nine o'clock; sometimes, indeed, later, but never earlier. It was then exactly half-past eight, and before my father had returned his watch into his pocket, one of my sisters exclaimed, "Here he is!" and we heard the wheels coming up the avenue. We should have heard him before, but two of my sisters were practicing a duet, which was to be produced at the approaching festivity, and drowned the sound.

Thereupon, I and my mother left the room, and went towards the back door, where Healy had just alighted, and was bringing sundry packages into the kitchen.

"Have you got my bat, Healy?" said I.

"No, sir," he replied. "There wasn't one in the whole town the size you wanted, but I'll bring you one from S. as I pass tomorrow. I know they've got 'em there. I believe that's all, Ma'am?" he added, addressing my mother.

She said she believed it was, and was going to pay him his week's account, which she had asked for, but he hurried out, saying, "Another time, if you please, Ma'am. I'm rather late to-night," and he was in his cart and away before I had time to give him some directions in regard to the bat.

"What a hurry he's in!" I said, "and it wants almost twenty minutes to nine now."

"I suppose he has a great many places to stop at," said my mother. "If he don't get all his parcels delivered before people are gone to bed, he gets into trouble sometimes. He's a very punctual fellow certainly."

We returned to the drawing-room, and resumed our occupations, and about half an hour afterwards, happening to be all silent at the moment, we heard a pair of light wheels and a brisk trotting horse passing in the road.

"That's farmer Gould's mare, I'm sure," said I. "What a famous trotter she is!"

"Yes," said my father. "I wish he'd part with her. I made him an offer the other day. I should like her for my buggy."

"And what did he say? Won't he sell her?"

"He said nothing. He only laughed, and shook his fat sides."

"Money is no object to him," said my mother. "He won't part with her unless he gets another he likes better."

We breakfasted at nine o'clock, and I was getting up, and about half-dressed, when one of my sisters burst into my room, crying, "La! Fred, such a shocking thing has happened! Poor Farmer Gould was found dead in the road this morning. They think his horse ran away, for it's not to be found, and the chaise[25] was upset and lying on its side. How lucky papa did not get the mare!"

"Who says so?" said I.

"The postman," she answered. "He saw some laborers standing round something in the road, and when he came up to them, he found it was the chaise, and poor farmer Gould quite dead beside it!"

When I got downstairs I found the whole house occupied with the subject of this sad accident, all lamenting the good man, who was a general favorite, and agreeing that, for so heavy a person, a two-wheeled carriage was very dangerous, as a fall was almost sure to be fatal.

My father said when he had finished his letters and papers he would walk up to the farm, and see if he could be of any use to poor Mrs. Gould. I, with the curiosity of fifteen, begged to go with him, and my mother improved the occasion by giving the governor a serious lecture about his love for high-trotting horses and buggies.

I expected Healy with my bat about eleven o'clock. As he had nothing else to bring, I knew he wouldn't come up the avenue, but leave it at a cottage near our gate, and wishing to learn if he'd heard any particulars about the accident, I walked down to meet him when the hour approached. Presently, I saw him coming, sitting in front of his cart.

"Well, Healy," I said. "Isn't this a shocking thing about poor Farmer Gould? You've heard he was found dead in the road this morning?"

"Yes, Sir, the mare ran away, and pitched him out upon his head. I can't say as ever I liked her myself. But I've got your bat, Master Frederick, a nice 'un too. I wouldn't come away this morning 'til I'd got it."

I thanked him, and he drove on, as if he had no time to lose in gossip, while I was untying the string of my parcel.

By the time my father and I reached Gould's farm, the doctor had arrived from B., and we heard he was examining the body in the parlor,

---

[25] One of various models of horse-drawn carriage, usually with a retractable open top, seating one or two people.

where it had been laid by the laborers who found it. The chaise, too, was standing near the door, just as it had been wheeled up, and the mare, they told us, had been found in a neighboring field, with the harness hanging about her, and unhurt, except on the forehead, where she appeared to have had a violent blow. The farm men, standing about, said that she had no doubt taken her head, and ran foul of something, and so pitched out Mr. Gould, and overturned the chaise, which seemed likely enough.

My father said he should like to see Mr. Wills, the surgeon, so we stood about outside 'til he came. When he did, he looked very grave, as, indeed, befitted the occasion. But in answer to my father's inquiries, he said that he could give no decided opinion of the cause of death 'til he had investigated the case further, and then he proceeded to examine the chaise, and next the horse. He then walked with us down to the spot where the thing had happened, and narrowly surveyed the ground, but he was very uncommunicative, which, as we knew him well, rather surprised us. He hurried away, saying, that he must prepare for the inquest on the following day.

My father went to the inquest, and I should have liked to go, too, but I was engaged to play a match at cricket with a few of my young neighbors. However, I was home first, for the inquest lasted a long time, and took a very unexpected turn.

It appeared that Mr. Wills, who was by marriage a connection of Gould's wife, had suspected on the first examination of the body that the farmer had not come fairly by his end. It so happened that Gould had dined with him the last day he was at B., and had mentioned to him that he had "at last got that seventy pounds that he was afraid he should never see," alluding to some money that had been long owing to him. As he spoke, he drew from his pocket a bundle of notes, some of which appeared to be of the Bank of England, and some of country banks. As soon, therefore, as Wills had arrived at certain conclusions, he inquired of Mrs. Gould if she had found his money safe.

In her grief and surprise, it had not occurred to her to search, and indeed she was not aware of his having any sum of importance about him. They proceeded immediately to examine his pockets, but no notes were there. A few shillings, a silver watch, and some unconsidered trifles were all that was found about him. Mr. Wills made inquiries at the banker's and others, at B., and by the time the inquest sat he was prepared to say that there was every reason to think that Mr. Gould had had this money in his waistcoat pocket, where he had seen him deposit it, at the time he left to return home.

This presented quite a new view of the case to the coroner, who had come there without the slightest suspicion of anything beyond an accident. The laborers were examined as to the attitude in which they had discovered the body, which, they all agreed, was lying on its face, and indeed there were some stains from the dirt of the road, which testified to this being the case. Yet, according to Mr. Wills, death had been occasioned by a terrible blow on the back of the head, which had fractured the skull, and which, in his opinion, was inflicted by a heavy bludgeon. The man's hair was very thick behind, but on dividing it a wound was visible, from which a small quantity of blood had oozed and dried up.

After a long investigation, the inquest was adjourned for a few days in order that further evidence might be collected. We were all much excited about this affair. It formed the staple of conversation at our dinner party, and various were the conjectures formed as to who was the criminal, if criminal there were, for some thought it possible that Gould had fallen on his back in the first instance, and then got upon his legs, and fallen a second time on his face. But Mr. Wills was confident the death wound was not the result of a fall, and besides, where was the money? Then all agreed that if he had been robbed, it was by no ordinary thief. It must have been by someone who knew the sum he had in his pocket, and who did not care for the loose silver and the watch.

"No doubt," said my father, "they will find out if anybody was present when the money was paid to him, or he may have told somebody of it, as he told Wills."

We had so many things provided for the party, that for two or three days we wanted nothing of Healy and did not see him, but the servants having mentioned that they wanted soap for the next week's washing, my mother sent a note to the cottage, where he always stopped to enquire for orders, desiring him to bring some on his return, and also a barrel of beer for the use of the kitchen.

When I heard the cart coming up the avenue, I went to the back door, to have a little gossip.

"Well, Healy," said I, as he rolled in the barrel of beer. "Have you heard any news?"

"'No, sir," said he.

"Nothing about farmer Gould?' I asked.

"No, sir, nothing. Shall I put the beer in the cellar?" he enquired.

This question being answered, I said, "Did you meet anybody on the road that night?"

"Lord, sir, I meet loads of people as I never take any notice of. I've enough to do to mind my own business."

"You couldn't have been far off when he was attacked, for you know Mr. Wills says he's been killed by a blow on the back of the head, don't you?"

"Well, sir, I've heard so, but how should he know? He wasn't there, I suppose. Anything else wanted, sir?"

"I believe not, Healy," I said, and he got into his cart and drove away. while I went back to the drawing-room.

"What does Healy say?" asked my father. "Has he heard anything new about this affair?"

"No, he says he hasn't, but he said very little and seemed rather sulky, I thought."

"By the bye, he couldn't have been far off when the thing happened, for he had only been gone half an hour when we recognized the step of poor Gould's mare, I recollect, and she'd soon overtake him."

"So I told him, and I asked him if he had met anybody on the road that night, but he said he'd plenty to do to mind his own business."

My father, who was reading the paper at the time, looked up at me over his spectacles, and then fell into a reverie that lasted some minutes, but he said nothing. My mother observed that she thought Healy ought to be summoned as a witness, and my father rejoined that no doubt he'd be examined.

On the following day the inquest was resumed. My father went early and had some private conversation with Mr. Wills, and I waited outside amongst the assembled crowd, listening to their speculations and conjectures. Presently, the coroner arrived, and I went in with him and heard the whole of the evidence. That of Mr. Wills, and the laborers who found the body was the same as before. Then, as my father had conjectured, Healy was called.

His face was familiar to everybody in the room, and there was not one I should think who was not struck with the singularly sulky, dogged expression his features had assumed. There was no manifest reason for it, for he was only summoned like other witnesses, and no breath of suspicion had been cast upon him, at least, as far as we had heard. But he evidently came in a spirit of resistance and wound up for self-defense.

He declared that he had not overtaken Mr. Gould on the night in question, and did not know he was on the road, nor did he hear anything of what had happened 'til the next morning. He believed he had met some tramps on the road that night -- two men and a woman -- but he had not particularly noticed them, and he did not recollect meeting anybody else. He had first heard of the accident at a shop where he had gone to buy a bat for Master C. When he said this, he looked up at me and our eyes met. I have often thought of that look since.

The next witness was Mr. F., who had paid Gould the seventy pounds in notes; and then a Mr. H. B., a solicitor, came forward and volunteered the following evidence, which, he said, he should have given before, but that he had left home on the afternoon preceding this unfortunate business, and had only returned yesterday. He was acquainted with Gould, and had met him at the door of the bank at B--, as he himself was on his way to the coach that was starting for E---.

Gould spoke to him, and said he had just got that seventy pounds, and when he said so, he clapped his hand on his pocket, implying it was there. He said, "I came to pay it in here, but I see they're shut, and it does not signify. I shall have to pay away a good deal of it next week." This was all that passed, as I told him I must be off for I should lose the coach.

Upon this, he was asked if anybody else had been present when Gould made this communication. He answered that people had been passing to and fro, but he could not say whether they heard it. There was one person who he thought might, though he could not affirm that he did, and that was Healy, the carrier, who was standing at the door of the tanner's shop, which is next to the bank, and examining some cricket bats that he had in his hand. Gould had spoken loud, as was his wont.

I saw Mr. Wills and my father exchange looks when this evidence was given, and then for the first time the question occurred to me: could Healy be the murderer? I could hardly entertain the suspicion -- it is so difficult to believe such a thing of a person one is having constant intercourse with. Healy was recalled and asked if he remembered seeing Mr. Gould and the lawyer together on that day. He declared he did not.

The harness was afterwards produced, and it appeared that the traces had been cut, which was a strong confirmation of the worst suspicions.

The inquest was once more adjourned, and Healy plied his trade as usual for the next two days, though everybody had a strange feeling towards him, and he retained his dogged, sulky look. On the third night we missed him. We had expected a parcel from B---, but he did not come, and the next day we heard he had been arrested on suspicion of being the murderer of Mr. Gould.

A gentleman's servant, who had been out without leave to some festivity at B---, and had come home and got in at the pantry window without being discovered, at last came forward, and said, that as he was going to the rendezvous, he had seen a cart, which he believed to be Healy's, though it was very dark, drawn right across the road. The horse was out of the shafts and tied to a gate, for he nearly ran against him. He did not see any person with the cart, but the driver might be behind it. It was just where there are some large trees over-hanging the road, which made it darker than in other parts, and a person driving would not see the obstruction 'til he was on it.

He himself, thinking it was Healy, slipped quietly by, for he did not want to be recognized, as the carrier often came to his master's, and might have betrayed him. He met a one-horse carriage about a couple of miles further on; the horse was trotting pretty fast. He thought it was Mr. Gould, but he could not positively say, as the night was so dark.

The spot described was precisely where Mr. Gould's body was found, and the man added, that it struck him when he met the gig, that if the cart had not moved out of the way, there would be an accident, and he should have warned the driver to look out, if he had not been upon a lark himself.

You may imagine the sensation created by this allegation in the neighborhood, where the carrier was so well known. 'Til the spring assizes[26] at E---, where he was to be tried, it furnished the staple of conversation, and every fresh bit of evidence, for or against him, was eagerly repeated and canvassed. My father was summoned as a witness to the hour at which Healy had been at our house that night, and also to recognizing the foot of Mr. Gould's mare. The evidence was entirely circumstantial, as nobody had witnessed the murder, though murder there certainly had been, nor was there anybody else to whom suspicion could attach. As for the tramps Healy said he had met, no trace of them could be found, nor did anyone appear to have seen such a party.

When all the evidence had been heard, my father said he felt considerable doubt what the verdict would be, and he really believed the jury were greatly perplexed, but when Healy stood up, and in the most solemn manner said, "I am innocent, my Lord! I call God to witness, I am innocent! May this right arm wither if I murdered the man!" So great an impression was made on the court, that, added to the prisoner's previous good character, everybody saw he would be acquitted.

He was. Healy went forth a free man, and we were all too glad to believe in his innocence, to dispute the justice of the verdict, but lo!

---

[26] English courts held at certain times of year, overseen by circuit court judges.

The hand of the Lord was on him. He had called upon God to bear witness to his words, and he did. In three days from that time, Richard Healy's stalwart right arm was withered! The muscles shrunk, the skin dried up, and it looked like the limb of a mummy!

Though a voice from Heaven testified against him, he could not be arraigned again for the same crime, and he remained at liberty. He attempted for a short time to carry on his business, but people ceased to employ him, and his feeble arm could no longer lift the boxes and hampers with which his cart was wont to be loaded. He went about, avoided by everyone but his own immediate connections. I often met him, but he never looked me in the face. Indeed, he rarely, if ever, raised his eyes. His round shoulders grew rounder, 'til he came to stoop like an old man. He seemed to move under a heavy burthen that weighed him to the earth.

After an interval, however, he bought some property, and in his old age -- for he survived his trial several years -- he was in prosperous circumstances. But everybody said, "Where did he get the money?"

We were all deeply interested in this singular story, and in reference to the withered arm, Colonel C. said that he should certainly not have believed it had he not seen it himself.

"I think," said I, "that it was not so difficult to account for the phenomenon as at first appears. Had he been innocent, the solemn adjuration he uttered in court would have been justifiable in the eyes of God and man, and would have occasioned him no concern afterwards. But he was guilty. He had called upon God to bear witness to a lie, and, doubtless, the consciousness of this sacrilegious appeal filled him with horror and alarm. He would tremble lest his prayer should be heard and the curse fall upon him. These terrors would direct all his thoughts to his arm, and produce the very thing he feared, for Sir Henry Holland[27] asserts that the mind is capable of acting upon the body to such a degree, as sometimes to create disease in a particular part on which the attention is too intently fixed."

---

[27] Holland (1788-1873) was a writer and medical doctor. He wrote about "the influence of the mind on the bodily organs," for example in his 1852 book *Chapters on Mental Physiology*.

Round the Fire
Fourth Evening

"The circumstance I am going to mention," said Sir Charles L.,
"will appear very insignificant after these interesting narratives, but as
it happened very lately, you'll perhaps think it worth hearing:

I was living a few months ago in a hotel, the owner of which died
while I was there. He had an apoplectic seizure, and expired shortly
afterwards. A week before this happened, at a time he was supposed to
be in perfect health, an acquaintance of the family called, and without
giving any reason, requested his daughter not to attend a ball she was
engaged to go to. The young lady did not take her advice, but the
visitor confided to another person that she had a particular reason for
her request, which reason was as follows.

The night before she called, she and her husband had retired to bed
in a somewhat anxious state of mind respecting a near relative of theirs,
who was very ill, and whom they had been visiting. The husband,
however, soon fell asleep, but the wife lay thinking of the sick person,
and the consequences that would ensue if she died, when her reflections
were interrupted by seeing a bright spot of light suddenly appear upon
the wall, that is, upon the wainscoat[28] of her room.

She looked about to see whence it proceeded; there was no light
burning, nor could any be reflected from the window. As she looked, it
increased in size, 'til, at last, it was as large as the frame of a picture.
Then there began to appear in the frame a form, gradually developed,
'til there was a perfect head and face, hair and all, distinctly visible.

Whilst this development was proceeding, she lay, as it were,
transfixed; she wanted to wake her husband, but she could neither
speak nor move. At length she seemed to burst the bonds, and cried to
him to look, but as she spoke, the vision faded, and by the time he was
sufficiently aroused there was nothing to be seen.

Both he and she interpreted this occurrence into a bad omen for
their sick relative, and augured very ill of her case, but the next
morning, as she was standing in her shop, she saw the hotel keeper pass
to market, and he nodded to her, whereupon she turned to her husband,
and exclaimed, "That's the face I saw last night! Sure nothing can be
going to happen to him!"

I heard these circumstances from my servant, and the unexpected
seizure and death occurred within a few days.

---

[28] Wooden paneling on the bottom few feet of a wall.

"When I was at Weimar,[29] about two years ago," said Mademoiselle G., "an accident occurred that occupied the attention of the whole place, and which seems to belong to the same class of phenomena as the story just related:

The palace, called the Château, in Weimar, is at one end of the park, and at the other end is another château, called the Belvedere.[30] Both are ducal residences, and an avenue runs from the one palace to the other. Opposite this avenue is the Russian chapel or Greek church, the present Dowager Duchess being a sister of the Emperor Nicholas,[31] and in front of this chapel a sentinel is always posted.

The Grand Duke, Charles Frederick,[32] father of the present sovereign, was, at the period I allude to, residing at the Belvedere not well in health, but by no means alarmingly ill, for had that been the case he would have been brought into Weimar, where etiquette requires that the sovereign should make his first and last appearance in this world -- there he must be born, and there die, if possible.

One night the sentinel, who was standing at the entrance of the Russian chapel, was surprised to see, in the far distance, a long procession winding its way down the avenue from the Belvedere. As there was no stir in the town, for the night was far advanced, and as he had not heard of any solemnity in preparation, the man stared at it in mute wonder, but his amazement was redoubled when it approached near enough for him to distinguish the individual objects to perceive that it was a State funeral, accompanied by the royal mourners, and all the pomp usual at these ceremonies.

The velvet pall[33] bore the initials and arms of the duke, and following the bier was his favorite and well-known horse, led by one of his attendants. Slowly and mournfully the procession moved on 'til it reached the chapel. The doors opened to admit the cortege;[34] it passed in; and as the doors closed on this mysterious vision, the soldier fell to the ground, where he was found in a state of insensibility when the guard was relieved.

---

[29] A German city, known for its arts and culture, later the namesake of the Weimar Republic.

[30] The "Schloss Belvedere" was a summer residence for the Duke of Saxe-Weimar.

[31] Probably Tsar Nicholas I, 1796 – 1855.

[32] Grand Duke of Saxe-Weimar-Eisenach, who lived from 1783 – 1853.

[33] A piece of fabric draped over a coffin.

[34] A funeral procession.

Of course, nobody believed his story. He was placed under arrest, severely punished, and had a nervous fever that brought him to the brink of the grave.

"I was there when this happened," said Mademoiselle G. "And it was the talk of the town. Almost everybody laughed at him, but five days afterwards the Duke fell suddenly ill, and was found to be in so dangerous a state, that the physicians forbade his being removed into the town. He finally died at the Belvedere, and was buried in the Russian chapel, exactly in the manner portrayed by the shadowy forms seen by the sentinel, and there buried."

We all agreed that these rehearsals, if we may so call them, are amongst the most perplexing of these very perplexing phenomena. A very curious case of this description will be found in one of the letters inserted in the Appendix.

"My sister-in-law, Lady S.," said Lady R., "told me, the other day, that during her late residence in St. Petersburg, she was intimately acquainted with a Prussian lady of high rank, to whom the following strange events occurred, an account of which she herself gave to my sister:

This Prussian lady was sitting one morning in her boudoir, when she heard a rustling sound in the ante-room, which was divided by a *portière*[35] from the boudoir. The sound continuing, she rose and drew aside the curtain to ascertain the cause, when, to her surprise, she saw a very pale man, in a Chasseur's[36] uniform, standing in the middle of the room. She was about to speak to him, and inquire what he was doing there, when he retreated towards the window and vanished.

Greatly alarmed, she sought her husband, and related what had occurred, but he laughed at her, and desired her not to expose herself to ridicule by talking of it. Some days afterwards, whilst in the boudoir, she heard the same rustling noise near her, and on looking up, she saw the figure of the Chasseur suspended in the air between the ceiling and the floor, with his legs dangling in the air.

A scream brought her husband, who was in the adjoining room, and he saw the figure as well as herself. Nevertheless, the fear of ridicule kept them silent, but some time afterwards, when they had a party, one of the company exclaimed, "Good Heavens! This, I remember, is the very room that unfortunate Chasseur hung himself in!" And then they

---

[35] A door.
[36] A French cavalry officer.

learned that the house had been previously occupied by the Danish minister, and that a Chasseur in his service had, from some cause or other, committed suicide.

"I don't know whether dreams are admissible," said Miss M. "But the sort of occurrences just related appear to me to be little removed from waking dreams. I know two cases of extraordinary dreaming, the authenticity of which I can answer for, if you would like to hear them." We accepted gladly, and the lady began as follows:

My father was intimate with Mr. S., whose name, perhaps, is known to you as the particular friend of Mr. Spencer Percival.[37] This gentleman, Mr. S., when he was a young man, had one night a remarkable dream, that he could not in any way account for, the circumstances having no relation to any previous event, train of thought, or conversation whatever.

He found himself, in his dream, on horseback, in a very extensive forest. He was alone, evening was drawing on, and he sought some place where he could pass the night. After riding a little farther, he espied an inn; he rode up to it and alighted, asking if they could give him lodging for the night, and stabling for his horse.

They said "Yes," and conducted him to an upper chamber. He ordered some refreshments, when it occurred to him that he should like to see how his horse was faring, and he descended, in order to find his way to the stables. In doing so, he got a glimpse of some very ill-looking men in a side chamber, who seemed in close conference; moreover, he thought he saw weapons lying on the table, and there were other circumstances which I do not precisely remember, the effect of which was to create alarm, and lead him to suspect he had fallen into a *repaire de voleurs*.[38]

He saw his horse rubbed down and fed, and then re-ascended to take his refreshment, betraying no suspicion of evil, but secretly resolved on flight. After his supper, he went down again, stood at the door, and pretended to stroll about. When he saw an opportunity, he went round to the stable, saddled his horse, and cautiously rode away. But he had not gone far, when he heard the tramp of horses' feet behind him, and from the pace they came, he felt sure he was pursued.

He urged his horse forward, but the animal was not fresh. He had done his day's work already, and the pursuers were gaining on him,

---

[37] Spencer Perceval (1762-1812) became the British Prime Minister in 1809, and was assassinated in 1812.

[38] Den of thieves.

when he saw he was approaching a spot where two roads met. Which of the two should he follow? He had nothing to guide him in his choice, and his life probably depended on his decision!

Suddenly, a voice whispered in his ear, "Take the right!" He did so, and shortly reached a house where he obtained shelter and protection.

When he awoke, the circumstances of his dream were so vividly impressed on his mind, that he could hardly believe the thing had not actually happened. He related it to his friends, and, for some days, thought a good deal of it, but he was just entering into active life, and the impression soon faded before the varied interests that absorbed him, and the strange dream was entirely forgotten.

Many years afterwards, when he had reached middle age, he was travelling in Germany, and in the course of an excursion he was making to see the country, he had occasion to cross a part of the Schwarzwald,[39] the Black Forest. He was on horseback and alone; he reached an inn, the aspect of which he fancied was familiar to him. Here he thought he might conveniently pass the night, so he alighted, ordered his supper, and then went to see his horse fed.

On further acquaintance with the place, he did not like the look of it, and he saw suspicious-looking men hanging about. He resolved to seek another resting-place, and leaving some money on the table to pay for what he had had, he went downstairs, and after lounging about a little, strolled to the stable, saddled his horse, and rode off as quietly as he could. But he was missed and pursued.

He heard the tramp of the horses as they gained upon him. At this critical moment, he saw he was approaching a place where the roads divided. His life depended on which of the two he should take. Suddenly, and strange to say, though he had misty recollections of the scene, now for the first time, the dream of his youth clearly and vividly recurred to him. He remembered the voice that whispered, "Take the right!"

He obeyed the hint, and his pursuers soon gave up the chase. He found a château about half a mile from the turning, the owner of which hospitably received him. His host said there had been for some time unpleasant suspicions with regard to the inn in question, and that, if he had taken the left-hand road, he would have been quite at their mercy.

This very curious dream reminded us of that of Dr. W., which I have related in the *Night Side of Nature*,[40] who in the same manner was

---

[39] The Black Forest, a large mountainous area of southwest Germany.
[40] This incident is found in Chapter V, "Warnings."

saved from the attack of an infuriated bull, in his dream, having been shown where to fly for safety, but the case is less remarkable than that of Mr. S., as the dream occurred only the night before the danger presented itself.

"The other dream I alluded to," said Miss M., "is less curious on that account:

Some friends of mine, who reside in the country, had an old nurse who had lived in the family many years, and for whom they had a great regard. When her services ceased to be required, she was settled in a cottage on the estate, where she lived very comfortably with her only daughter. The daughter, however, married a man who kept a turnpike[41] some miles distant, and one morning, just as the family was leaving home on some expedition, the old woman arrived in considerable agitation, saying that she had had a frightful dream about her daughter, and that she was going off immediately to the place where she lived.

The ladies endeavored to dissuade her from walking all that way, merely on account of a dream. But she said she could not rest, and must go. They even promised that, if she would wait 'til the following day, they would drive her there in the carriage, in which there was now no room. If there had been they would have taken her, as their road lay not far from the spot.

With this offer they left her and went their way, but her anxiety would not permit her to wait, and shortly afterwards she set off and walked all the distance to the turnpike. The moment she arrived she saw reason to rejoice in her determination.

She found her daughter alone, her husband having been called away on business, and, said the young woman, "I am dreadfully alarmed, for there is a quantity of money in the house. The farmers are accustomed to bring the money for their rent here twice a year, as it saves them several miles, and the agent always comes to fetch it on the same day. But a letter to my husband has just arrived from the agent to say he can't come 'til tomorrow. Knowing his hand, I opened it, and I am terrified, for the custom of leaving the money here is no secret, and if it should get wind that it has not been fetched away, heaven knows what may happen."

The old woman then told her daughter that she had dreamed on the preceding night that some thieves had broken into the turnpike house, and robbed and murdered the inhabitants.

---

[41] A toll road.

But what were these two helpless women to do, mutually confirmed in their apprehensions as they naturally were? It was already late in the day, there was no help near at hand, and besides, they did not dare to separate in search of any. They watched anxiously for a traveler, resolved to confide in the first respectable one that passed, and beg him to send assistance. But none came that they thought it safe to trust.

Night approached, and it being a little frequented road, except on market days, every moment their hope of help declined. So they did the best they could in this extremity. They shut and barricaded the lower part of the house, stopping up the door and windows with every piece of furniture they had, and locked themselves up, with the money, in an upper chamber, put out the light, and with a chink of the window open, they set themselves down to listen for the marauders whom they confidently expected to arrive.

Nor were they disappointed. About eleven o'clock their anxious ears distinguished the sound of approaching footsteps. Presently, they heard voices and the door was attempted. The men said they had lost their way, and on receiving no answer they attempted to force an entrance. Then, the poor women knowing their poor defenses would soon yield to violence, began to scream lustily from the window above, and luckily not in vain.

It happened that the family, who had gone on some expedition of pleasure in the morning, was just then returning. Their road lay within a quarter of a mile of the turnpike, and in the silence of the night, the women's shrill voices reached their ears. They immediately desired the coachman to turn his horses' heads in the direction the cries came from, and before the thieves had affected an entrance into the little fortification, they were scared by the sound of approaching wheels and took to flight.

"A dream of a very singular nature occurred to a young friend of mine," said Mr. S. "She was about fifteen at the time, and a schoolfellow who was going to be married had promised her that she should be one of the bridesmaids. The intended wedding was near at hand, insomuch that the dresses and everything was prepared. In short, the fixing of the day was only delayed by some small matter of business that was not completed.

"My young friend, to whom the whole thing was an exciting novelty, while impatiently waiting for the affair to come off, dreamed, one night, that a person, in a very unusual costume, presented himself at her bedside and informed her that he was Brutus,[42] and that he would reveal to her anything that she particularly desired to know, whereupon she begged him to tell when Miss L. would be married.

"Brutus answered '*Paulo post Græcas Kalendas.*'[43] When she awoke in the morning, she perfectly remembered the words, but not having the most distant idea of their meaning, she ran to her brother to enquire if he could explain them. He told her that they were equivalent to 'never.' The prophecy was fulfilled; obstacles entirely unforeseen arose, and the couple were never united."

"Some years ago," said Dr. Forster, "two young friends of mine were staying at Naples, when one of them told the other that he had on the preceding night seen, in his sleep, the face of a beautiful woman. But the features were disfigured by a horrible expression, and it was, somehow, impressed on his mind that he was in danger, and he must be on his guard against her. The conviction was so strong as to create considerable uneasiness, and he never went out without scrutinizing every female face he saw, but some weeks passed without any fulfilment of his dream or vision, and gradually the impression faded.

"However, he was one day on the Chiaja,[44] surrounded by several people who, like himself, were observing a gang of convicts going to the Castle of St. Elmo,[45] when something occasioned him suddenly to turn his head, and there, close behind him, he recognized the beautiful face of his dream.

"By an instinctive impulse, he sprang aside, and at the same moment felt himself wounded in the back. The woman was seized and did not attempt to deny the act, but alleged that she had mistaken the young Englishman for another person who had done her an irreparable injury, expressing great regret at having wounded an unoffending stranger, and also at having failed in the revenge she sought. He told me that the dream saved his life, for that, had he not sprung aside, the wound would in all probability have been mortal."

---

[42] Marcus Junius Brutus, famous for his role in the assassination of Julius Caesar.

[43] Soon after the Greek Kalends. In the Roman calendar, the first day of the month. The Greeks had no equivalent specific day, so the expression meant something was being postponed indefinitely.

[44] A street in Naples, Italy, usually seen spelled Chiaia.

[45] The Castel Sant'Elmo, a medieval fortress above Naples.

Round the Fire
Fifth Evening

"I have but one experience to relate," said Miss D., the next speaker:

When I was a child, I and my elder sister slept in two beds, placed close beside each other. We were in the country, and one night my father, going to the door, perceived an unusual light in the sky, and learnt on inquiry that there was a great fire a mile or two off. He said he'd go to see it, and the night being fine, my mother accompanied him, having first seen us safe in bed. She locked the chamber door, and took the key, thinking that everybody would be out looking at the fire, and we might take the opportunity of playing tricks, for we were quite young at the time -- not more than six or seven years old.

After they were gone, we lay chattering, as children do, about our own little concerns, when our voices were suddenly arrested by terror. At the foot of my bed I perceived a figure, apparently kneeling, for I saw only the head, but that I saw distinctly. It looked dark and sad, and the eyes were intently fixed on me.

I crept into my sister's bed, and neither of us dared to look up again until my mother returned, and came to see if we were asleep. We had not closed our eyes, and we told her what we had seen, agreeing perfectly in our account of it. The room was searched, but nothing unusual found. The incident made a lasting impression on my sister and myself, and we both remember the face as if we had seen it but yesterday.

One of the ladies present mentioned a very similar circumstance occurring to herself, but as she was alone at the time, she had always endeavored to believe it an illusion.

"The first part of the story I am going to relate to you," said Dr. S., "was told me by an eminent man in my own profession, who had every opportunity of testing the truth of it. The latter part I give you on my own word:

Some years ago there was a house in the suburbs of Dublin that had remained a long time unoccupied, in consequence, it was said, of its evil reputation: the report was that it was haunted. People who had taken it got rid of it as soon as they could, and those who lived in the neighborhood affirmed that they saw lights moving about the interior, and, sometimes, a lady in white standing at the window with a child in her arms, when they knew there was no living creature, except rats and mice, within the walls. The wise and learned laughed at these rumors, but still the house remained empty, and was getting into a very dilapidated state.

The former owner of the house was dead. He was a miser or a misanthrope, or both. At all events, for several years he had lived in it utterly alone, and scarcely ever seen by anybody. It was rumored that for a short time a young female had been occasionally observed by the neighbors, but she disappeared as suddenly as she had appeared, and nobody knew whence she came, nor whither she was gone. His life was a mystery, and whether merely on this account, or whether there were better grounds for it, there had certainly existed a prejudice against him.

However, as I said, he had been dead some years, and the relative to whom the property had fallen on his decease was naturally very anxious to let the house, and offered it to any occupant at an extremely low rent.

At length, a gentleman who wanted to establish a manufactory, seeing that it would answer his purpose -- for the premises were extensive, and there was some garden ground behind -- took it, and erected buildings on this waste ground for his workmen to inhabit. Between the new part and the old there was a long vestibule, or covered passage, by which they might pass from one to the other without exposing themselves to the weather. A large door, which was open by day and closed at night, divided this passage in two, and on one side there was a small room or office, where a clerk sat and kept the books and memoranda, of various sorts, incident to a considerable business.

However, the thing was scarcely set going and established before it reached the ears of the master that the workmen objected to pass the night on the premises. The reason alleged being that they were disturbed and alarmed by various sounds, especially footsteps, and the banging of the heavy door in the vestibule which divided the sleeping places from the workrooms.

At first, the objection being thought absurd, was not attended to. Next, it was supposed to be a trick of some of the workmen to frighten the others. But when it became serious, and they began to act upon it, and steady, respectable men declared they heard these things, the master, still persuaded it was some practical jokers amongst them mystifying the more simple, took measures, first, to ascertain if such sounds as they described were audible, and next, to discover who made them. For this purpose he sat up himself, and his clerks sat up, and exactly as had been described, at one o'clock this clatter and banging of doors commenced. That is, there was the sound, for the doors remained immovable, and though they heard footsteps they could see nobody.

"Still," said the manufacturer, who was not willing to be made the victim of this mischievous conspiracy, "we must discover who it is, and we shall, when they are more off their guard." For this purpose it was arranged that a relation of his own, a young man in whose discretion and courage he had great confidence should sleep in the office.

Accordingly, a bed was prepared there, and he arranged himself for that night or as many future nights as it might be necessary, determined not to relinquish the investigation until he had unraveled the mystery.

At dawn of day, the next morning, there was a violent knocking at the outer door. An early passenger had found this young man in the street, with nothing on but his night dress, and in a state of delirium. He was taken home and Dr. W. was sent for. The result was a brain fever, but when he recovered, he said that he had gone to bed and to sleep, that he was wakened by a loud noise, and that just as he was about to rise to ascertain the cause, his door opened, and the apparition of a female dressed in white entered, and approached his bedside. He remembered no more, but being seized with horror, supposed he had got out of the window into the street, where he was found.

This was, certainly, very extraordinary and very serious. Still the persuasion that it was some mystification prevailed, and Dr. W.'s offer to pass a night in the office himself, was gladly accepted. He had informed me of the young man's illness and the cause of it, and when I heard of his intention, I requested leave to bear him company.

The noise had not been interrupted by the catastrophe that had occurred, and nobody had slept in the office during the young man's confinement. The bed had been removed, but we declined having it re-placed, for we wished our intention to remain a secret; besides, we preferred watching through the night. It was not until the workmen had all retired that we took up our position, accompanied by a sharp little terrier of mine, and each armed with a pistol.

We took care to go over the house, to make sure that nobody was concealed in it, and we examined every door and window to ascertain that it was secure. We had provided ourselves with refreshments also, to sustain our courage, and we entered upon our vigil with great hopes of detecting the imposition.

Dr. W. is a most enlightened and agreeable companion, and we soon fell into a lively discussion that carried us away so entirely, that, I believe, we had both ceased to think of the object of our watch, when we were recalled to it by the clock in the vestibule striking one, and the loud bang that immediately followed, accompanied by the barking of our little dog, who had been aroused from a tranquil sleep by the uproar.

W. and I seized our pistols, and rushed into the passage, followed by the terrier. We saw nothing to account for the noise, but we distinctly heard receding footsteps, which we hastened to pursue, at the same time urging on the dog, but instead of running forward, he slunk behind, with his tail between his legs, and kept at our heels the whole way. On we went, distinctly hearing the footsteps preceding us along the vestibule, down some steps, and, finally, down some stairs that led to an unused cellar, in one corner of which lay a heap of rubbish. Here the sound ceased. We removed the rubbish, and under it lay some bones, which we recognized at once as parts of a human skeleton. On further examination, we ascertained that they were the remains of a female and a newborn infant.

They were buried, and the men were no more disturbed with these mysterious noises. Who the woman was, was never ascertained, nor was any further light thrown upon these strange circumstances.

Some remarks on the terror displayed by animals, on these occasions, elicited a curious story from Mrs. L. "They not only seem to see sometimes," she said, "what we do not, but occasionally to be gifted with a singular foreknowledge:

Many years ago, I and my husband went to pay a visit in the north. I am very fond of animals, and my attention was soon attracted by a dog that was not particularly handsome, but seemed gifted with extraordinary intelligence.

"I see," said my hostess, "you are struck with that dog. Well, he is the most mysterious creature. He not only opens and shuts the door, and rings the bell, and does all sorts of wonderful things, but I am sure he understands every word we say, and that he knows as well what I am saying now as you do. Moreover, we got him in a very unaccountable manner.

"One night, not long ago, we had been out to dinner, and on returning at a pretty late hour, we found the gentleman stretched out comfortably on the dining-room rug.

"'Where in the world did this dog come from?' I said to the servants.

"They couldn't tell; they declared the doors had been long shut, and that they had never set eyes on him 'til that minute.

"'Well,' I said. 'Don't turn him out. He'll no doubt be claimed by someone in the neighborhood.' For he had quite the manners and air of a dog accustomed to good society, and I liked his large, expressive eyes. He made himself quite at home, and now we have discovered what a strangely intelligent creature he is, I hope no one will claim him, for I should be very sorry to part with him. But," added she, "poor Mrs. X. can't endure him."

Mrs. X., I must mention, was a widow lady, also on a visit there, with an only son.

"Why?" said I.

"It is rather singular, certainly," said she, "but whenever young X. is in the room, the dog never takes his eyes off his face. You see he has peculiar eyes -- they're full of meaning -- and out of doors he does the same."

"Perhaps the dog has taken a fancy to him?" I suggested.

"It does not seem to be that. No, I think he likes me and Mrs. C. and my children a great deal better. I can't tell what it is, but if you watch, you'll see it."

I did, and it was really remarkable, and evidently annoyed Mrs. X. very much. The young man affected to laugh at it, but I don't think he liked it altogether.

Suddenly, one evening, Mrs. X., whose visit was to have extended to some weeks longer, announced that she should take her departure in a few days. I suspected this move was occasioned by her desire to get away from the dog, and so did my hostess, and we both thought it absurd.

Mr. L. being obliged to return to London, we took our leave the morning after this announcement was made, but we had scarcely arrived there, when a letter from my friend followed, informing me that young Mr. X. had been unfortunately drowned in the fishpond, and that the dog had never been seen since the accident, though they had made inquiries and sought for him in every direction. Whence he came, or whither he went, they were never able to discover.

"But," said Mrs. L., "as this is not a ghost story, I will tell you another anecdote that belongs more legitimately to the subjects you are treating of:

Once, when we were travelling in the North, Mr. L. fell ill of a fever at Paisley.[46] This detained us there, and the minister called on us. When Mr. L. recovered, we returned his visit, and, in the course of

---

[46] A town in the Scottish Lowlands.

conversation, some of the old customs of the Scotch fell under discussion, amongst others the cutty stool,[47] which we had heard still subsisted.

"Why don't you abolish it?" said Mr. L. "It would be much better to amend people by other influences than exposure."

"Well, sir," said the good man. "That was my opinion also, and I had determined to do it. Before taking the step, however, I thought it advisable to publish my reasons, and I was one day sitting at the table writing on the subject, when I looked up, and beheld my father, who was minister here before me, and died in this manse, sitting on the opposite side of the table."

"'Don't do any such thing, David,' said he. 'Morality is loose enough; don't make it looser.'"

---

[47] A stool set up in a Scottish church, where people would sit for public shame or penance.

Round the Fire
Sixth Evening

"The most interesting circumstance of the ghostly kind that I know, as really authentic," said Madame S., "is what happened to the late Lord C., when he was a young man. It is an old story, and you must have heard of the Radiant Boy,[48] but as I had it from a member of the family, perhaps you will accept it as my contribution:

Captain S., who was afterwards Lord C.,[49] when he was a young man, happened to be quartered in Ireland. He was fond of sport, and one day the pursuit of game carried him so far that he lost his way. The weather, too, had become very rough, and in this strait he presented himself at the door of a gentleman's house, and sending in his card, requested shelter for the night.

The hospitality of the Irish country gentry is proverbial. The master of the house received him warmly, said he feared he could not make him so comfortable as he could have wished, his house being full of visitors already. Added to which, some strangers, driven by the inclemency of the night, had sought shelter before him, but that such accommodation as he could give he was heartily welcome to. Whereupon he called his butler, and committing his guest to his good offices, told him he must put him up somewhere, and do the best he could for him. There was no lady, the gentleman being a widower.

Captain S. found the house crammed, and a very jolly party it was. His host invited him to stay, and promised him good shooting if he would prolong his visit a few days, and, in fine, he thought himself extremely fortunate to have fallen into such pleasant quarters.

At length, after an agreeable evening, they all retired to bed, and the butler conducted him to a large room, almost divested of furniture, but with a blazing peat fire in the grate, and a shake down[50] on the floor, composed of cloaks and other heterogeneous materials.

Nevertheless, to the tired limbs of Captain S., who had had a hard day's shooting, it looked very inviting, but before he lay down, he thought it advisable to take off some of the fire, which was blazing up

---

[48] A generic term for the glowing ghost of a murdered boy, usually murdered by a parent.

[49] The blog *Seeks Ghosts* identifies this as Robert Stewart (1760-1822), who would become Viscount Castlereagh. He served on the cabinet of the Prime Minister the Duke of Portland, along with Spencer Perceval, mentioned in the Fourth Evening.

[50] A bed made up on the floor.

the chimney, in what he thought, an alarming manner. Having done this, he stretched himself upon the couch, and soon fell asleep.

He believed he had slept about a couple of hours when he awoke suddenly, and was startled by such a vivid light in the room, that he thought it was on fire, but on turning to look at the grate he saw the fire was out, though it was from the chimney the light proceeded. He sat up in bed, trying to discover what it was, when he perceived, gradually disclosing itself, the form of a beautiful naked boy, surrounded by a dazzling radiance. The boy looked at him earnestly, and then the vision faded, and all was dark.

Captain S., so far from supposing what he had seen to be of a spiritual nature, had no doubt that the host, or the visitors, had been amusing themselves at his expense, and trying to frighten him. Accordingly he felt indignant at the liberty, and on the following morning, when he appeared at breakfast, he took care to evince his displeasure by the reserve of his demeanor, and by announcing his intention to depart immediately.

The host expostulated, reminding him of his promise to stay and shoot. Captain S. coldly excused himself and, at length, the gentleman seeing something was wrong, took him aside, and pressed for an explanation, whereupon Captain S., without entering into particulars, said that he had been made the victim of a sort of practical joking that he thought quite unwarrantable with a stranger.

The gentleman considered this not impossible amongst a parcel of thoughtless young men, and appealed to them to make an apology, but one and all, on honor, denied the impeachment. Suddenly, a thought seemed to strike him; he clapped his hand to his forehead, uttered an exclamation, and rang the bell.

"Hamilton," said he to the butler. "Where did Captain S. sleep last night?"

"Well, Sir," replied the man, in an apologetic tone. "You know every place was full -- the gentlemen were lying on the floor, three or four in a room -- so I gave him the Boy's Room, but I lit a blazing fire to keep him from coming out."

"You were very wrong," said the host. "You know I have positively forbidden you to put anyone there, and have taken the furniture out of the room to ensure its not being occupied."

Then retiring with Captain S., he informed him very gravely of the nature of the phenomenon he had seen, and, at length, being pressed for further information, he confessed that there existed a tradition in his family, that whoever the Radiant Boy appeared to will rise to the summit of power, and when he had reached the climax, will die a violent death, and I must say, he added, that the records that have been kept of his appearance go to confirm this persuasion.

"I need not remind you," said Madam S., "what a remarkable confirmation was afforded by the life and death of Lord C."[51]

"I had never heard these particulars before; but I had heard the story of Lord C.'s Radiant Boy alluded to, *ápropos* of the case of the Reverend Mr. A., who saw a very similar apparition some years ago at C. Castle. I have related this case in the *Night Side of Nature*.[52] I received the particulars from a relation of Mr. A.'s, who was himself surviving at the time I published it."

"It is curious," observed Mrs. E., "how many houses in the north of England where I have been lately residing have something of this sort attached to them:

Some friends of mine not long ago heard of a very pretty place to let, and finding the rent unusually moderate they took it. They were delighted with their new residence, and often wondered that the proprietor, with whom they were slightly acquainted, did not either live there himself, or insist on more money for it.

After they had been there some time, his brother, that is, the brother of the proprietor, who did not live very far off, called one morning to see them, and asked them how they liked the place. They expressed their extreme satisfaction, adding, "We wonder your brother does not live here himself."

"There are reasons why it does not suit our family," he answered.

When he was going away, my friends proposed to walk through the grounds with him. They had to cross a little brook not far from the house, and as they did so, a hare sprang past them and they all stopped and turned round to look at her, by which means they had a full view of the house.

"Good Heavens!" exclaimed the visitor. "There she is!"

"Where?" enquired my friend, thinking he alluded to the hare.

"Is any of your family ill?" asked the stranger.

"No," they answered, and following the direction of his eyes, they observed at one of the upper windows of the house, a female figure in white, and enveloped in what looked like grave clothes.

---

[51] In the last year of his life, Castlereagh began to suffer from paranoia and a general mental decline, leading to his suicide.

[52] This incident is found in Chapter XIV, "Spectral Lights, and Apparitions attached to Certain Families."

The visitor appearing much agitated, my friend rushed back and ran up to the floor where the female had appeared, and not only was there no one there, but he found that the window was that of a vestibule and much too high from the ground for anyone to reach.

On returning to their visitor, he said, "One of us will die before this year has expired. It is an unfailing omen in our family, and caused us so much distress, that that is the real reason why we do not live here. But it concerns nobody but ourselves. You will never be troubled by her visitations." The destiny fell on the seer himself this time; he was dead before the year had expired.

There is another house in the same part of the county, where some time ago a young friend of mine, one of three sisters, went on a visit for a short time. The first night, after she got into bed, she was startled by the most terrific screams she ever heard, which appeared close to her door. She jumped up and opened it, but there was nobody there.

The next day she mentioned the circumstance, but the old lady she was visiting said her ears must have deceived her, and turned the conversation, but she heard it again several times, and was quite sure there was no mistake. When she went home she told her sisters, who laughed at her, but each of them went to visit subsequently at the same house and heard precisely the same thing, but as it was evidently an unpleasant subject to their hostess, they could get no information on the subject.

"A near relation of mine," said Lord N., "is living in a place at present, where there is very much the same annoyance, and three families successively had left the house in consequence of it:

The building is large, part of it very old, and it is surrounded by a fine park. Nevertheless, it has been found difficult to get a tenant -- or, at least, to keep one. My relation was warned of the inconvenience before he took it. It is said that a lady was murdered there by her husband.

At all events, there is one room -- one of the best in the house, shut up, and never allowed to be opened. Whoever sleeps in the room under this is liable to be disturbed by extraordinary noises, footsteps and moving of furniture, and etc. But the most strange thing is, that every now and then a dreadful piercing scream is heard through the house, that brings any strangers who happen to be there out of their rooms, in terror, to enquire what has occurred. The family who resided there before met the apparition of a lady occasionally, and left the place in consequence. My relations have never seen anything, but everybody who stays there any time hears the screams.

Another relation of mine, a very religious person, and as she belongs to the Free Church of Scotland,[53] most opposed to the belief in ghosts, went some time since to pay a visit at an old place belonging to our family. On the morning after her arrival, she announced at breakfast that she was going away. She gave no reason, but went, to the consternation of her host.

With much difficulty, he has since extracted from her that in the night an apparition appeared at the foot of her bed, a man dressed in an old-fashioned brown suit. He spoke to her, and some conversation passed, the subject of which she declares she will never disclose. She says it was not a good spirit, and nothing would induce her to visit the place again. This house has always been said to be haunted, but this is the only instance I know of the family themselves seeing anything of the sort, but no better evidence could be adduced of such a phenomenon than that of the lady in question. Nobody ever doubted her word, and a more confirmed disbeliever in ghosts never existed.

"A rather curious thing happened to myself lately," continued Lord N.:

I went to visit some friends at the Lakes.[54] As they had no vacant rooms, I engaged apartments near them for myself and servant. The house was small, quite modern, and as unghostly as possible. I always dined with my friends, and went to my lodgings about twelve o'clock, and I had been there five or six nights without anything unusual occurring.

On the fourth or fifth evening, I had returned home rather earlier than usual, and instead of going to bed, I sat down to write a letter. While so engaged, I heard what I thought was a boy cracking a whip close to the drawing-room door. I paid no attention to it at first, though rather wondering at the hour chosen for the amusement. However, as it continued un-intermittingly, and grew louder, I got up and opened the door, with the intention of desiring the child to go away. There was no one there.

It then occurred to me that my ears must have deceived me, and that the sound might have proceeded from some explosive substance in

---

[53] Denomination begun after the Disruption of 1843, separated from the Church of Scotland.

[54] Presumably the Lake District, a scenic area familiar from the poetry of Wordsworth and Coleridge.

my bedroom fire. The room was on the same floor, and the door shut, but when I opened it, I found the fire almost out, certainly not in a state to produce the noises I had heard.

I went forward to stir it, and while doing so, the whip was cracked over my shoulder. I turned round quickly, but could see nothing, and I returned to the drawing-room, and had just seated myself again, when I was amazed to see the table rise about a foot perpendicularly into the air, and at the same moment, both the candles that were on it went out, without being upset or even moved. There was a fire, so that I was not quite in the dark, and I relighted them, after which the whip began cracking again vigorously, and cracked on until I went to bed and afterwards. I stayed in these apartments a fortnight or three weeks longer, and once, again, I heard the whip, but much fainter and for a shorter time, and one night there were distinct rappings on the mantelpiece, and afterwards on the dressing-table.

I could make no discovery in regard to these phenomena, and I leave it to the company to decide whether they were of a spiritual nature or not. The only other thing of the sort that ever happened to me was this: I was travelling on the Continent, and not being very well, was lying in bed, when I suddenly saw the door open, and two of my brothers walk through the room, dressed in deep mourning. I rang the bell furiously, and the people came, but could in no way explain what had happened. I shortly received letters, announcing that another brother had died at that time.

I will mention another instance that occurred in our family a few years since. During my grandfather's last illness, all the family was assembled at K. Castle, except my brother John, with whom he was not on good terms. While we were living there, waiting to see what turn the illness would take, John died very unexpectedly, but we resolved not to mention the circumstance to Lord A., as it might affect him injuriously. It was therefore kept a profound secret.

One day, some little time afterwards, Lord A. had been asleep in his armchair, and on waking, he suddenly exclaimed, "I shall see John on Thursday!"

This was on a Monday, and he died on the Thursday following.

"A relation of mine," said Mrs. L., "had a friend with whom a great intimacy had subsisted for many years, but a subject of difference arose that embittered her feelings towards this lady to such a degree, that she felt reconciliation impossible. They continued to live in the same town, but all intercourse was at an end.

"One morning, lately, she was lying awake in her bed, when the door opened, and this lady came in. Approaching the bedside, she spoke in a friendly manner, and entered into explanations with regard to the misunderstanding. My relation was not frightened during this interview, but when it was over, and she was gone, she suspected the nature of the visit. When her maid came to her room, she enquired if there had been any news of Miss ---. The servant answered, none, but presently afterwards, a person called to mention the lady's death, which had taken place that morning."

"For my part," said Sir A. C., "I am acquainted with a circumstance that has settled entirely any doubts I might have entertained on the subject of ghosts:

Not many miles from my place in S---shire, there is a seat belonging to some connections of my own. At the time I am about to refer to, an old lady was in possession, and it so happened, that a matter of business arose regarding the heirs of the property, which made it necessary to refer to the title deeds. To the surprise and dismay of the family, they could not be found. A vigorous search was instituted, in vain, and the circumstance so preyed on my old relation's mind that she at length committed suicide, under the impression that someone else would lay claim to the estate.

After her death people complained that they could not live there. The place, they said, was haunted by this old lady, who, with her grey hair disheveled, and dressed exactly as she used to be in her lifetime, they described as walking about the house, looking into drawers and cupboards, and incessantly searching for her deeds. We, of course, did not believe in the story, and were not even altogether convinced when the house, after being let to several strangers in succession, who all gave it up on the same plea, seemed destined to remain without an inhabitant.

It had stood empty two or three years, though offered at a very low rent, when a lady and gentleman from the West Indies came into the neighborhood to visit some acquaintance, and being in want of a residence, and hearing this was to be had on very reasonable terms, they proposed to take it. Their friends told them of the objection made by preceding tenants, but they laughed with scorn at the idea of losing so good a house on account of a ghost, so they closed the bargain, took possession of the place, and sent for their family to join them.

The children, the youngest of whom was between three and four, and the eldest about ten, were, as a temporary arrangement, placed on the first night of their arrival to sleep in one room. But the next morning, when their mother went at a very early hour to see how they were, to her surprise, she found them all wide awake. They were looking pale and weary, and began with one voice to complain that they had been kept awake all night by such a disagreeable old lady, who would keep coming into the room, and looking for something in the drawers.

"I told her I wished she'd go away," said the eldest, "and then she did go; but she came back; and we don't like her. Who is she, mamma? Is she to live with us?"

"They then, on being questioned, described her appearance, which exactly coincided with the account given by the former tenants. I can vouch for the truth of these circumstances, and since these children had, certainly, never heard a word on the subject of the apparition, and had, indeed, no idea that it was one, I think the evidence," said Sir A. C., "is quite unexceptionable."

"I should say so, too, if it referred to any other question," said Mr. E., a barrister, who happened to be present when the story was related. "But on the subject of ghosts I cannot think any evidence sufficient."

"A state of mind by no means uncommon," I said, "and which it is, of course, in vain to contend with. I can only wonder and admire the confidence that can venture to prejudge so interesting and important a subject of inquiry."

Round the Fire
Seventh Evening

"My story will be a very short one," said Mrs. M., "for I must tell you that though, like everybody else, I have heard a great many ghost stories, and have met people who assured me they had seen such things, I cannot, for my own part, bring myself to believe in them. But a circumstance occurred when I was abroad, that you may perhaps consider of a ghostly nature, though I cannot:

I was travelling through Germany, with no one but my maid. It was before the time of railways, and on my road from Leipsic to Dresden,[55] I stopped at an inn that appeared to have been long ago part of an aristocratic residence. A castle, in short, for there was a stone wall and battlements, and a tower at one side, while the other was a prosaic-looking, square building that had evidently been added in modern times. The inn stood at one end of a small village, in which some of the houses looked so antique that they might, I thought, be coeval with the castle itself.

There were a good many travelers, but the host said he could accommodate me, and when I asked to see my room, he led me up to the towers, and showed me a tolerably comfortable one. There were only two apartments on each floor, so I asked him if I could have the other for my maid, and he said yes, if no other traveler arrived. None came, and she slept there.

I supped at the *table d'hôte*,[56] and retired to bed early, as I had an excursion to make on the following day, and I was sufficiently tired with my journey to fall asleep directly.

I don't know how long I had slept, but I think some hours, when I awoke quite suddenly, almost with a start, and beheld, near the foot of the bed, the most hideous, dreadful-looking old woman, in an antique dress, that imagination can conceive. She seemed to be approaching me, not as if walking, but gliding, with her left arm and hand extended towards me.

"Merciful God deliver me!" I exclaimed, under my first impulse of amazement, and as I said the words she disappeared.

"Then, though you don't believe in ghosts, you thought it was one when you saw it," said I.

---

[55] Two large cities in the German region of Saxony.
[56] Hotel restaurant.

"I don't know what I thought. I admit I was a good deal frightened, and it was a long time before I fell asleep again.

"In the morning," continued Mrs. M., "my maid knocked, and I told her to come in, but the door was locked, and I had to get out of bed to admit her. I thought I might have forgotten to fasten it. As soon as I was up, I examined every part of the room, but I could find nothing to account for this intrusion. There was neither trap or moving panel, or door that I could see, except the one I had locked. However, I made up my mind not to speak of the circumstance, for I fancied I must have been deceived in supposing myself awake, and that it was only a dream, more particularly as there was no light in my room, and I could not comprehend how I could have seen this woman.

"I went out early, and was away the greater part of the day. When I returned, I found more travelers had arrived, and that they had given the room next mine to a German lady and her daughter, who were at the *table d'hôte*. I therefore had a bed made up in my room for my maid, and before I lay down, I searched thoroughly, that I might be sure nobody was concealed there.

"In the middle of the night -- I suppose about the same time I had been disturbed on the preceding one -- I and my maid were awakened by a piercing scream, and I heard the voice of the German girl in the adjoining room, exclaiming, '*Ach! meine mutter! meine mutter!*'[57]

"For some time afterwards I heard them talking, and then I fell asleep, wondering, I confess, whether they had had a visit from the frightful old woman. They left me in no doubt the next morning. They came down to breakfast greatly excited, told everybody the cause, described the old woman exactly as I had seen her, and departed from the house incontinently, declaring they would not stay there another hour."

"What did the host say to it?" we asked.

"Nothing. He said we must have dreamed it, and I suppose we did."

"Your story," said I, "reminds me of a very interesting letter which I received soon after the publication of *The Night Side of Nature*. It was from a clergyman who gave his name, and said he was chaplain to a nobleman. He related that in a house he inhabited, or had inhabited, a lady had one evening gone upstairs, and seen, to her amazement, in a room, the door of which was open, a lady in an antique dress, standing before a chest of drawers, and apparently examining their contents.

"She stood still, wondering who this stranger could be, when the figure turned her face towards her, and, to her horror, she saw there

---

[57] "Oh, my mother! My mother!"

were no eyes. Other members of the family saw the same apparition also. I believe there were further particulars, but I unfortunately lost this letter, with some others, in the confusion of changing my residence.

"The absence of eyes I take to be emblematical of moral blindness, for in the world of spirits there is no deceiving each other by false seemings. As we are, so we appear."

"Then," said Mrs. W. C., "the apparition, if it was an apparition, that two of my servants saw lately, must be in a very degraded state:

There is a road, and on one side of it a path, just beyond my garden wall. Not long ago two of my servants were in the dusk of the evening walking up this path, when they saw a large, dark object coming towards them. At first, they thought it was an animal, and when it got close, one of them stretched out her hand to touch it. But she could feel nothing, and it passed on between her and the garden wall, although there was no space, the path being only wide enough for two, and on looking back, they saw it walking down the hill behind them. Three men were coming up on the path, and as the thing approached, they jumped off into the road.

"Good heavens, what is that!" cried the women.

"I don't know," replied the men. "I never saw such a thing as that before."

The women came home greatly agitated, and we have since heard there is a tradition that the spot is haunted by the ghost of a man who was killed in a quarry close by.

"I have traveled a great deal," said our next speaker, the Chevalier de La C. G., "and, certainly, I have never been in any country where instances of these spiritual appearances were not adduced on apparently credible authority:

I have heard numerous stories of the sort, but the one that most readily occurs to me at present, was told to me not long ago, in Paris, by Count P., the nephew of the celebrated Count P., whose name occurs in the history of the remarkable incidents connected with the death of the Emperor Paul.[58]

Count P., my authority for the following story, was attached to the Russian embassy, and he told me, one evening, when the conversation

---

[58] Paul I of Russia (1754-1801) was son of Catherine the Great. Two Count P.s were implicated in the conspiracy that led to his assassination: Peter Ludwig von der Pahlen and Nikita Petrovich Panin.

turned on the inconveniences of traveling in the East of Europe, that, on one occasion, when in Poland, he found himself about seven o'clock in an autumn evening on a forest road, where there was no possibility of finding a house of public entertainment within many miles. There was a frightful storm; the road, not good at the best, was almost impracticable from the weather, and his horses were completely knocked up.[59]

On consulting his people what was best to be done, they said that to go back was as impossible as to go forward, but that by turning a little out of the main road, they should soon reach a castle where possibly shelter might be procured for the night. The count gladly consented, and it was not long before they found themselves at the gate of what appeared a building on a very splendid scale. The courier quickly alighted and rang at the bell, and while waiting for admission, he enquired who the castle belonged to, and was told that it was Count X's.

It was some time before the bell was answered, but at length an elderly man appeared at a wicket,[60] with a lantern, and peeped out. On perceiving the equipage, he came forward and stepped up to the carriage, holding the light aloft to discover who was inside. Count P. handed him his card, and explained his distress.

"There is no one here, my lord," replied the man, "but myself and my family. The castle is not inhabited."

"That's bad news," said the count. "But nevertheless, you can give me what I am most in need of, and that is shelter for the night."

"Willingly," said the man. "If your lordship will put up with such accommodation as we can hastily prepare."

"So," said the count, "I alighted and walked in, and the old man unbarred the great gates to admit my carriages and people. We found ourselves in an immense *couer*,[61] with the castle *en face*,[62] and stables and offices on each side. As we had a *fourgon*[63] with us, with provender for the cattle and provisions for ourselves, we wanted nothing but beds and a good fire, and as the only one lighted was in the old man's apartments, he first took us there.

They consisted of a suite of small rooms in the left wing, that had probably been formerly occupied by the upper servants. They were comfortably furnished, and he and his large family appeared to be very well lodged. Besides the wife, there were three sons, with their wives

---

[59] Exhausted.
[60] A small gate alongside a larger gate.
[61] Heart. Here it seems to imply a courtyard.
[62] In front.
[63] A van or truck, used for carrying goods.

and children, and two nieces, and in a part of the offices, where I saw a light, I was told there were laborers and women servants, for it was a valuable estate, with a fine forest, and the sons acted as *gardes chasse.*[64]

"Is there much game in the forest?" I asked.

"A great deal of all sorts," they answered.

"Then I suppose during the season the family live here?"

"Never," they replied. "None of the family ever reside here."

"Indeed!" I said. "How is that? It seems a very fine place."

"Superb," answered the wife of the custodian. "But the castle is haunted."

She said this with a simple gravity that made me laugh, upon which they all stared at me with the most edifying amazement.

"I beg your pardon," I said. "But you know, perhaps, in great cities, such as I usually inhabit, there are no ghosts."

"Indeed!" said they. "No ghosts!"

"At least," I said, "I never heard of any, and we don't believe in such things."

They looked at each other with surprise, but said nothing, not appearing to have any desire to convince me. "But do you mean to say," said I, "that that is the reason the family don't live here, and that the castle is abandoned on that account?"

"Yes," they replied. "That is the reason nobody has resided here for many years."

"But how can you live here then?"

"We are never troubled in this part of the building," said she. "We hear noises, but we are used to that."

"Well, if there is a ghost, I hope I shall see it," said I.

"God forbid!" said the woman, crossing herself. "But we shall guard against that. Your *Seigneurie*[65] will sleep not far from this, where you will be quite safe."

"Oh! But I am quite serious," I said. "If there is a ghost, I should particularly like to see him, and I should be much obliged to you to put me in the apartments he most frequents."

They opposed this proposition earnestly, and begged me not to think of it. Besides, they said if anything was to happen to my lord, how should they answer for it? But as I insisted, the women went to call the members of the family who were lighting fires and preparing beds in some rooms on the same floor as they occupied themselves.

---

[64] Gameskeepers.
[65] Your Lordship.

When they came they were as earnest against the indulgence of my wishes as the women had been. Still I insisted.

"Are you afraid," I said, "to go yourselves in the haunted chambers?"

"No," they answered. "We are the custodians of the castle and have to keep the rooms clean and well aired lest the furniture be spoiled -- my lord talks always of removing it, but it has never been removed yet -- but we would not sleep up there for all the world."

"Then it is the upper floors that are haunted?"

"Yes, especially the long room. No one could pass a night there; the last that did is in a lunatic asylum now at Warsaw," said the custodian.

"What happened to him?"

"I don't know," said the man. "He was never able to tell."

"Who was he?" I asked.

"He was a lawyer. My lord did business with him, and one day he was speaking of this place, and saying that it was a pity he was not at liberty to pull it down and sell the materials, but he cannot, because it is family property and goes with the title. The lawyer said he wished it was his, and that no ghost should keep him out of it. My lord said that it was easy for anyone to say that who knew nothing about it, and that he must suppose the family had not abandoned such a fine place without good reasons.

"But the lawyer said it was some trick, and that it was coiners,[66] or robbers, who had got a footing in the castle, and contrived to frighten people away that they might keep it to themselves. So my lord said if he could prove that he should be very much obliged to him, and more than that, he would give him a great sum, I don't know how much. So the lawyer said he would, and my lord wrote to me that he was coming to inspect the property, and I was to let him do anything he liked.

"Well, he came, and with him his son, a fine young man and a soldier. They asked me all sorts of questions, and went over the castle and examined every part of it. From what they said, I could see that they thought the ghost was all nonsense, and that I and my family were in collusion with the robbers or coiners. However, I did not care for that. My lord knew that the castle had been haunted before I was born.

"I had prepared rooms on this floor for them -- the same I am preparing for your lordship -- and they slept there, keeping the keys of the upper rooms to themselves, so I did not interfere with them. But one morning, very early, we were awakened by someone knocking at our

---

[66] Counterfeiters.

bedroom door, and when we opened it, we saw Mr. Thaddeus -- that was the lawyer's son -- standing there half-dressed and as pale as a ghost, and he said his father was very ill, and he begged us to go to him.

"To our surprise he led us up stairs to the haunted chamber, and there we found the poor gentleman speechless, and we thought they had gone up there early and that he had had a stroke. But it was not so. Mr. Thaddeus said that after we were all in bed, they had gone up there to pass the night. I know they thought that there was no ghost but us, and that's why they would not let us know their intention.

"They laid down upon some sofas, wrapped up in their fur cloaks, and resolved to keep awake, and they did so for some time, but at last the young man was overcome by drowsiness. He struggled against it, but could not conquer it, and the last thing he recollects was his father shaking him and saying, 'Thaddeus, Thaddeus, for God's sake keep awake!'

"But he could not, and he knew no more until he woke and saw that day was breaking, and found his father sitting in a corner of the room speechless, and looking like a corpse, and there he was when we went up. The young man thought he'd been taken ill or had a stroke, as we supposed at first, but when we found they had passed the night in the haunted chambers, we had no doubt what had happened: he had seen some terrible sight and so lost his senses."

"He lost his senses, I should say, from terror when his son fell asleep," said I, "and he felt himself alone. He could have been a man of no nerve. At all events, what you tell me raises my curiosity. Will you take me upstairs and show me those rooms?"

"Willingly," said the man, and fetching a bunch of keys and a light, and calling one of his sons to follow him with another, he led the way up the great staircase to a suite of apartments on the first floor. The rooms were lofty and large, and the man said the furniture was very handsome, but old. Being all covered with canvas cases, I could not judge of it.

"Which is the long room?" I said.

Upon which he led me into a long narrow room that might rather have been called a gallery. There were sofas along each side, something like a dais[67] at the upper end, and several large pictures hanging on the walls.

I had with me a bulldog, of a very fine breed, that had been given me in England by Lord F. She had followed me up stairs -- indeed, she

---

[67] A raised platform.

followed me everywhere -- and I watched her narrowly as she went smelling about, but there were no indications of her perceiving anything extraordinary. Beyond this gallery there was only a small octagon room, with a door that led out upon another staircase. When I had examined it all thoroughly, I returned to the long room and told the man, as that was the place especially frequented by the ghost, I should feel much obliged if he would allow me to pass the night there. I could take upon myself to say that Count X. would have no objection.

"It is not that," replied the man, "but the danger to your lordship." And he conjured me not to insist on such a perilous experiment.

When he found I was resolved, he gave way, but on condition that I signed a paper, stating that in spite of his representations I had determined to sleep in the long room.

I confess, the more anxious these people seemed to prevent my sleeping there, the more curious I was. Not that I believed in the ghost the least in the world. I thought that the lawyer had been right in his conjecture, but that he hadn't nerve enough to investigate whatever he saw or heard, and that they had succeeded in frightening him out of his senses. I saw what an excellent place these people had got, and how much it was their interest to maintain the idea that the castle was uninhabitable. Now, I have pretty good nerves -- I have been in situations that have tried them severely -- and I did not believe that any ghost, if there was such a thing, or any jugglery by which a semblance of one might be contrived, would shake them.

As for any real danger, I did not apprehend it. The people knew who I was, and any mischief happening to me would have led to consequences they well understood. So they lighted fires in both the grates of the gallery, and as they had abundance of dry wood, they soon blazed up. I was determined not to leave the room after I was once in it, lest, if my suspicions were correct, they might have time to make their arrangements, so I desired my people to bring up my supper, and I ate it there.

My courier[68] said he had always heard the castle was haunted, but he dare say there was no ghost but the people below, who had a very comfortable berth of it, and he offered to pass the night with me, but I declined any companion and preferred trusting to myself and my dog. My valet, on the contrary, strongly advised me against the enterprise, assuring me that he had lived with a family in France whose château was haunted, and had left his place in consequence.

---

[68] A servant who took charge of travel arrangements.

By the time I had finished my supper it was ten o'clock, and everything was prepared for the night. My bed, though an impromptu, was very comfortable, made of amply stuffed cushions and thick coverlets, placed in front of the fire. I was provided with light and plenty of wood, and I had my regimental cutlass, and a case of excellent pistols, which I carefully primed and loaded in presence of the custodian, saying, "You see I am determined to fire at the ghost, so if he cannot stand a bullet, he had better not pay me a visit."

The old man shook his head calmly, but made no answer. Having desired the courier, who said he should not go to bed, to come upstairs immediately if he heard the report of firearms, I dismissed my people and locked the doors, barricading each with a heavy ottoman[69] besides. There was no arras[70] or hangings of any sort behind which a door could be concealed, and I went round the room, the walls of which were paneled with white and gold, knocking every part, but neither the sound, nor Dido, the dog, gave any indications of there being anything unusual. Then I undressed and lay down with my sword and my pistols beside me, and Dido at the foot of my bed, where she always slept.

I confess I was in a state of pleasing excitement. My curiosity and my love of adventure were roused, and whether it was ghost, or robber, or coiner, I was to have a visit from, the interview was likely to be equally interesting. It was half-past ten when I lay down. My expectations were too vivid to admit of sleep, and after an attempt at a French novel, I was obliged to give it up; I could not fix my attention to it.

Besides, my chief care was not to be surprised. I could not help thinking the custodian and his family had some secret way of getting into the room, and I hoped to detect them in the fact, so I lay with my eyes and ears open in a position that gave me a view of every part of it, 'til my travelling clock struck twelve, which being preeminently the ghostly hour, I thought the critical moment was arrived.

But no, no sound, no interruption of any sort to the silence and solitude of the night occurred. When half-past twelve, and one struck, I pretty well made up my mind that I should be disappointed in my expectations, and that the ghost, whoever he was, knew better than to encounter Dido and a brace of well charged pistols. But just as I arrived at this conclusion, an unaccountable *frisson*[71] came over me, and I saw Dido, who, tired with her day's journey, had lain 'til now quietly curled up asleep, begin to move, and slowly get upon her feet. I thought she

---

[69] An overstuffed, couch-like seat with no back.

[70] Tapestry.

[71] A thrill of excitement.

was only going to turn, but, instead of lying down, she stood still with her ears erect and her head towards the dais, uttering a low growl.

The dais, I should mention, was but the skeleton of a dais, for the draperies were taken off. There was only remaining a canopy covered with crimson velvet, and an arm chair covered with velvet too, but cased in canvas like the rest of the furniture. I had examined this part of the room thoroughly, and had moved the chair aside to ascertain that there was nothing under it.

Well, I sat up in bed and looked steadily in the same direction as the dog, but I could see nothing at first, though it appeared that she did. But as I looked, I began to perceive something like a cloud in the chair, while at the same time, a chill which seemed to pervade the very marrow in my bones crept through me. Yet the fire was good, and it was not the chill of fear, for I cocked my pistols with perfect self-possession and abstained from giving Dido the signal to advance, because I wished eagerly to see the denouement of the adventure.

Gradually, this cloud took a form, and assumed the shape of a tall white figure that reached from the ceiling to the floor of the dais, which was raised by two steps.

"At him, Dido! At him!" I said, and away she dashed to the steps, but instantly turned and crept back completely cowed. As her courage was undoubted, I own this astonished me, and I should have fired, but that I was perfectly satisfied that what I saw was not a substantial human form, for I had seen it grow into its present shape and height from the undefined cloud that first appeared in the chair.

I laid my hand on the dog who had crept up to my side, and I felt her shaking in her skin. I was about to rise myself and approach the figure, though I confess I was a good deal awestruck, when it stepped majestically from the dais, and seemed to be advancing.

"At him!" I said. "At him, Dido!" and I gave the dog every encouragement to go forward. She made a sorry attempt, but returned when she had got halfway and crouched beside me, whining with terror. The figure advanced upon me; the cold became icy; the dog crouched and trembled; and I, as it approached, honestly confess, that I hid my head under the bed clothes and did not venture to look up 'til morning.

I know not what it was -- as it passed over me I felt a sensation of undefinable horror, that no words can describe -- and I can only say that nothing on earth would tempt me to pass another night in that room, and I am sure if Dido could speak, you'd find her of the same opinion.

I had desired to be called at seven o'clock, and when the custodian, who accompanied my valet, found me safe and in my perfect senses, I must say the poor man appeared greatly relieved, and when I descended the whole family seemed to look upon me as a hero. I thought it only just to them to admit that something had happened in the night that I felt impossible to account for, and that I should not recommend anybody who was not very sure of their nerves to repeat the experiment.

When the Chevalier had concluded this extraordinary story, I suggested that the apparition of the castle very much resembled that mentioned by the late professor Gregory, in his letters on mesmerism,[72] as having appeared in the Tower of London[73] some years ago, and from the alarm it created, having occasioned the death of a lady, the wife of an officer quartered there, and one of the sentries. Everyone who had read that very interesting publication was struck by the resemblance.

---

[72] William Gregory (1803 – 1858), a Scottish chemist, wrote *Letters To A Candid Inquirer On Animal Magnetism* in 1851.

[73] "The Tower Ghost" appears as Case 65 in Gregory's *Animal Magnetism, or, Mesmerism and its Phenomena*.

Round the Fire
Eighth Evening

As this was our last evening, I was called upon for a story, but I pleaded that I had told all mine in the *Night Side of Nature*, and of personal experience I had very little to tell; but I said," I will give you the history of a visit I made several years ago to a haunted house, although it resulted in almost nothing:

After the publication of the *Night Side*, I received many valuable communications. I wish I had kept a note of them all, but I never expected to publish again on the same subject.

Amongst others, I received a letter from a gentleman called McN., and as it contained several interesting particulars, I requested him to call on me. I remember, in the letter, he told me that a few years previously, he had been on an excursion from home, and that while stopping at an inn, one morning, about five o'clock, the door opened and his father entered. He came to the bedside, looked at him, and then went out again. The young man sprang from his bed, and followed him downstairs, where he lost sight of him. He returned home, and found his father had died on that morning.

He was in a lawyer's office, and, amongst other things, he mentioned to me that there was, not very far off, a house said to be haunted, of which they had the charge, but that it was impossible to do anything with it.

"We offer it at a mere nominal rent, but no one will stay there."

I was often absent from home at this time, but for the next two or three years I sometimes met him and inquired about the house. The report was always the same until, at length, no one would go into it. It was shut up, the shutters were closed, and the boys of the neighborhood threw stones at the windows and broke the glass. Yet it was situated in a street where every other house was inhabited, and which had not been built many years.

It was as much as six or seven years after I had first heard of this house, that I happened to mention the circumstance to some gentlemen of my acquaintance, very eminent men, with honest, inquiring minds, truth-seekers, who, if she were in the bottom of a well, would have thought it right to go after her. As they had humility enough to feel that they could not pronounce upon a question that they had never studied or investigated, they expressed a wish to visit the house.

Accordingly, I applied to Mr. McN., who had the keys in his office, and he obligingly consented to accompany us. Our expedition was to be kept a profound secret, and it was so, until some time afterwards, when, like most other secrets, it got wind and it spread abroad.

We started in a carriage, between eleven and twelve o'clock at night, taking with us a young girl who was easily mesmerized, and when in that state a good clairvoyant. She was not told the object of our journey, and had no means whatever of learning it. We said we were going to look at a house, and that that was the most convenient time for the gentleman to show it us. We did not drive to the door, but Mr. McN. met us in the next street, where we alighted, lest we should attract observation.

We walked to our destination, and Mr. McN. explained to the policeman on duty who he was and where we were going, lest he should suspect mischief, and interrupt us. He then unlocked the door with the aid of the policeman's lantern, for it was a dark winter's night, and on entering, we found ourselves in a narrow passage.

It was a small house, in no respect different from the others in the street. They seemed all of the same description. A narrow frontage, with one window and the door, on the ground floor; two windows above; two rooms on a floor, three stories in height; and a kitchen, scullery, and cellars underground.

As soon as the door closed on us, we were in utter darkness, but we had provided ourselves with candles and matches, and when we had lighted them, we entered the back parlor, which Mr. McN. had heard from the different inhabitants was the room in which they had met with most annoyance.

The clairvoyant was then put to sleep, and asked if she liked the house, and would recommend us to take it. She shuddered and said, no, that two people had been murdered there, and we should be *troubled*.

We asked in which room; she answered, "It was before this house was built -- another house stood there then -- a very old house."

This was not exactly on the same ground, but the room we were in was on part of it. She said that it was these murdered people who would trouble us. We asked if she could see them, and she answered, "No."

We then waited in silence to see if anything occurred, but nothing did, except a metallic sound at the door, which was ajar, like the striking of two pieces of iron. We all heard it, but could not say what occasioned it.

After a little time, someone suggested that we should extinguish the lights. We did so, and were then in absolute darkness. There was but one window in the room, and that was coated with dust, and the shutter was shut. Besides, as I have said, it was a very dark night, and this room, being at the back, looked into a yard, I believe; at all events, not into a street.

Presently, the clairvoyant started, and exclaimed, "Look there!" We saw nothing, and asked what it was.

"There!" she said. "There again! Don't you see it?"

"What?" we asked.

"The lights!" she said. "There! Now!" These exclamations were made at intervals of two or three seconds.

We all said we saw nothing whatever.

"If Mrs. Crowe would take hold of my hand, I think she would see them," she suggested.

I did so, and then, at intervals of a few seconds, I saw thrown up, apparently from the floor, waves of white light: faint, but perfectly distinct and visible. In order that I might know whether our perceptions of this phenomenon were simultaneous, I desired her, without speaking, to press my hand each time she saw it, which she did, and each time I distinctly saw the wave of white light. I saw it, at these intervals, as long as I held her hand and we were in the dark. Nobody saw it but she and myself, and we did not follow up the experiment by the others taking her hand, which we should have done.

During this interval, another light suddenly appeared in the middle of the room, away from where we were standing. I saw a bright diamond of light, like an extremely vivid spark, only not the color of fire. It was white, brilliant, and quiescent, but shed no rays. I did not mention this, because I wished to learn if it was visible to anybody else, but nobody spoke of it, not even the clairvoyant. Whether she saw it or not, I cannot say.

When the candles were re-lighted, these lights were no longer visible. I and one of the gentlemen went over the house above and below, but saw nothing but the dust and desolation of a long uninhabited dwelling.

When we came away, and Mr. McN. had locked the door, we walked to the carriage. I said, "Then you none of you saw the waves of light."

"No," said they.

"Well," said I, "I certainly did, and I never saw anything like it before. Moreover, I saw another sort of light."

"Did you?" said Mr. McN., interrupting me. "Was it a bright spark of light like the oxy-hydrogen light?"[74]

---

[74] A mixture of oxygen and hydrogen gases was used in lamps, particularly the incandescent "limelight."

"'Exactly," said I. "I could not think what to compare it to, but that was it."

I thus was certain that he had seen the same thing as myself. He had not spoken of it from a similar motive; he waited to have his impression confirmed by further testimony.

You see our results were not great, but the visit was not wholly barren to me. Of course, many wise people will say I did not see the lights, but that they were the offspring of my excited imagination. But I beg to say that my imagination was by no means excited.

If I had been there *alone*, it would have been a different affair, for though I never saw a ghost nor ever fancied I did, I am afraid I should have been very nervous. But I was in exceedingly good company, with two very clever men, besides the lawyer, a lady, and the clairvoyant, so that my nerves were perfectly composed, as I should not object to seeing any ghost in such agreeable society. Moreover, I did not expect any result, because there is very seldom any on these occasions, as ghosts appear we know not why, but certainly not because people wish to see them. They generally come when least expected and least thought of.

Mr. Mc.N., on inquiry, learnt that unaccountable lights were amongst the things complained of. What occasioned them and the other phenomena, it had certainly been the proprietor's interest for many years to discover. It had also been the interest of numerous tenants, who having taken the house for a term, found themselves obliged to leave it at a sacrifice. Yet, for all those years, no explanation could be found for the annoyances but that the house was haunted. No tradition seems extant to account for its evil reputation. If what the clairvoyant said was true, the murders must have occurred long ago.

A gentleman, an inhabitant of the same city, once mentioned to me that a friend of his, many years previously, when quite a young man, had one Sunday evening been walking alone in the fields outside this town, and that he met a young woman, a perfect stranger, who, on some pretense asked him to see her safe home. He did so. She led him to a lone farmhouse, and then inviting him to walk in, showed him into a room and left him.

Whilst waiting for her return, idly looking about, he found hidden under the table, which was covered with a cloth, a dead body. On this discovery, he rushed to the door. It was locked, but the window was not very high from the ground, and by it he escaped, terrified to such a degree, that he not only left the city that very evening, but hastened out of the country, apprehensive that he had been enticed to the house and shut up with the murdered man, for the purpose of throwing the guilt on him. As justice was not so clear-sighted, and much more inexorable than in these days, he feared the circumstantial evidence might go against him. He settled in a foreign country and finally died there.

Where this locality was, I don't know, except that it was in the environs of the city, environs which have since been covered with buildings. What if the house that we visited should have been erected on the site of that lone farm?

It may be so. At all events, this story shows how possible it is that some similar event might have occurred on the spot where the haunted house stands.

In conclusion, let me once more recall to my readers that one, whose insight none will dispute, reminds us, in relation to this very subject, that "our philosophy,"[75] does not comprehend all wisdom and all truth. Philosophy is a good guide when she opens her eyes, but where she obstinately shuts them to one class of facts because she has previously made up her mind they cannot be genuine, she is a bad one.

Professor A. told me that when he was at Göttingen,[76] as a great favor, and through the interest of an influential professor there, he was allowed to see a book that had belonged to Faust, or Faustus,[77] as we call him. It was a large volume, and the leaves were stiff and hard like wood. They contained his magic rites and formulas, but on the last page was inscribed a solemn injunction to all men, as they loved their own souls, not to follow in his path or practice the teaching that volume contained.

There appears to be a mystery out of the domain, I mean the present domain of science, within the region of the hyper-psychical, regarding our relations, while in this world, with those who have passed the gates: a belief in which is, I think, innate in human nature. This belief, in certain periods and places, grows rank and mischievous; at others, it is almost extinguished by reaction and education. But it never wholly dies, because, everywhere and in all times, circumstances have occurred to keep it alive, amongst individuals, which never reach the public ear.

Now, the truth is always worth ascertaining on any subject, even this despised subject of ghosts, and those who have an inherent

---

[75] Allusion to the famous quote from *Hamlet*: "There are more things in heaven and earth, Horatio, than are dreamt of in your philosophy"

[76] A city in the Saxony region of Germany, renowned for its university.

[77] Famous as the protagonist of plays by Christopher Marlowe (1592) and Johann Wolfgang von Goethe (1832), many believe the character was based on a historical 15th century alchemist, Johann Georg Faust.

conviction that they themselves are spirits, temporarily clothed in flesh, feel that they have a special interest in the question. We are fully aware that the investigation presents all sorts of difficulties, and that the belief is opposed to all sorts of accepted opinions, but we desire to ascertain the grounds of a persuasion, so nearly concerning ourselves which in all ages and all countries has prevailed in a greater or less degree, and which appears to be sustained by a vast amount of facts, which, however, we admit are not in a condition to be received as anything beyond presumptive evidence. These facts are chiefly valuable, as furnishing cumulative testimony of the frequent recurrence of phenomena explicable by no known theory, and therefore as open to the spiritual hypothesis as any other.

When a better is offered, supported by something more convincing than pointless ridicule and dogmatic assertion, I for one, shall be ready to entertain it. In the meanwhile, hoping that time may, at length, in some degree, rend the veil that encompasses this department of psychology, we record such experiences as come under our observation and are content to await their interpretation.

Appendix

I have referred in the preceding pages to the loss of several letters, which I should have been glad to insert here.

The following very interesting ones I have fortunately retained. I give them verbatim, only suppressing the names of the writers, as requested.

Letter 1

August 18, 1854.

MADAM,

I have received your kind favor of the 15th, and I really feel that I must now apologize to you, for venturing so quickly to call in question the accuracy of your details. Being unaware, however, of the marvelous coincidence of the two dreams, I feel assured you at once appreciated the motives which alone impelled me to write.

Allow me, then, to attempt a narration of the particulars referred to in my last, as having come under my own observation.

Two intimate friends of mine, clergymen of the Church of England, and one of whom is unmarried, have for the last three years occupied a large old-fashioned house in the country. It is a very pretty place, stands within its own grounds, and is quite aloof from any other dwellings. It has long had the reputation in the neighborhood of being haunted, in consequence, it is said, of a former proprietor having committed suicide there.

The story goes thus: he was laid out in a chamber which is now called the spare room, and is the scene of what I am about to relate. I may as well tell you that it was only on my last visit, some six weeks since, that I became at all aware of the character of the mansion, for my friends felt so annoyed at what has taken place, that they purposely avoided communicating to their visitors what they thought might make them anything but comfortable.

On that occasion there happened to be on a visit to my friend's wife, a lady very nearly related to him. She had the spare room assigned to her as a chamber, and on the very first night of her arrival was so terrified by what took place that she would not again sleep there without company.

She stated that in the middle of the night she was alarmed by the most unearthly groanings and lamentations. The voice seemed close to her bedside. It was afterwards attended by a rustling noise, and she distinctly felt the curtains at the foot of the bed removed. Now, as my knowledge of what was going on could not be disputed, my friends admitted that it was not the first time these noises had been heard, nay, that in two instances the apparition of a form in grave-clothes had been seen: the one occurring to a young gentleman of about twenty years of age, who happened to be visiting them, and the other to one of their own servants.

In the former case, it appears that the young man was sitting rather late at night in the study reading, all the family being in bed, when the form emerged, apparently, from the wall dividing the study from the haunted chamber. It remained a short time only and then melted away. So great was the young man's terror that he has never been near the place since. The servant also described a similar appearance, and no one in the house who saw her terror could believe it acted.

Independently of all this, no less than four gentlemen, two of them from the University, have experienced all the unearthly groanings and be-wailings before mentioned, and in nearly every instance the parties were, like myself, ignorant of the character attributed to the house. But I now come to my own experience.

I was on a visit to my friends about twelve months since, when I met a gentleman who had just left the army for the church. He appeared about 21 years of age, and there was that indescribable *something* in his manner which charmed me immediately. Without any pretense to being set up, so to speak, in piety, there was yet that in his sunny countenance and air of cheerfulness, which made you feel that he had been called to a brighter path of usefulness. I certainly very much admired him, and I have since learnt that he is a general favorite. On retiring to rest I found that he was to occupy the next room; not the study side.

From a variety of causes I could not sleep, but the imaginative powers were not particularly aroused. My thoughts were of very prosy and worldly things. As near as I could recollect, about an hour after I had been in bed, I heard the most dreadful groans followed by exclamations of the most horrible kind. The voice certainly seemed in the room, and was continued for at least two hours, at intervals of about ten minutes. It was that of a man who had committed a deadly sin which could never be pardoned! The agony seemed to me to be intense.

Will you believe it, Madam? In spite of what I thought of my acquaintance of the next chamber, I ascribed it to him. I believed little in the supernatural, and concluded it to be some dreadful dream. It is astonishing the thought never struck me, that a continuous dream of such a character was scarcely possible. It did not, however, and despite of its unearthly character, and the apparent woe of the unfortunate one, the despair, as I said before, of a lost soul, I continued to associate it all with my neighbor next door, until the events which occurred at my last visit entirely upset my conviction, and I became at once assured I had been doing him a great injustice.

Like some of the cases in the *Night Side of Nature*, you will perceive here a great difference in the manifestations: to some it was given to *hear*, to others to *see*. Are you still of opinion that this results from what you term comparative freedom of rapport! Do you not think there are times when the material may give place to the supernatural? I admit freely the truth of spectral illusions -- I have myself experienced one -- but knew it to be nothing more. Still, notwithstanding this, and my further belief in a certain connection of mind and matter, I cannot altogether cast from me the persuasion that the Almighty One may at times think fit to exercise a power independent of all rule, for the attainment of certain ends to us, perhaps, unknown.

I cannot conclude without telling you that with regard to what I have mentioned above, nothing in the shape of trick could possibly have been practiced. Trusting I may not have trespassed too much on your patience, I will now remain, Madam, yours very respectfully,

J. H. H.

Letter 2

Gloucestershire, June 10, 1854.
MADAM,

Being not long ago on a visit of some days at the house of a friend, I happened to meet with your work, entitled *The Night Side of Nature*.

The title struck my imagination, and opening the book I was delighted to find that it treated of subjects which had long engaged my serious thoughts. I was much pleased to see in you such an able and earnest protester against the cold skepticism of the age in reference to truths of the highest order, and those too sustained by a body of evidence which in any other case would be esteemed irresistible.

I must also say that I never met with so great a number of well-authenticated facts in any other work as you have given us, whilst the truly catholic spirit of your theological reflections was to me peculiarly refreshing.

I once had a thought of making a similar collection. That design I have however abandoned, the state of my health not admitting of much literary labor. I could relate to you many things as remarkable as any you have described, for the truth of which I can vouch. I will mention one of a most singular nature, and should you be inclined to read anything more from me on these matters, I shall feel a pleasure in the communication. Writing letters I find to be a relief from a melancholy, induced some two years ago by a variety of heavy afflictions, and this must be my apology for addressing you. But to my narrative:

Shortly after I entered the ministry, I was introduced to a gentleman of very superior mind who belonged to the same profession, and whom I had never seen equaled for the genius and eloquence which his conversation displayed.

I became at once attached to him, and for some reason or other he evinced a desire to cultivate my friendship. After some months of most agreeable intercourse had elapsed, he was taken seriously ill, and one evening I was hastily summoned to his house. On my entering his chamber, he requested that we might be left alone, and he then told me that it was his impression that his disease was mortal; that many supernatural occurrences had marked his life, which he desired might be given to the world when he was gone; and that he wished me to perform this office.

Having expressed my willingness to gratify him, he commenced the chapter of extraordinaries. Here is one event in his remarkable history. Prior to his becoming a minister, and when in humble circumstances, he lodged at the house of a tradesman at a certain seaport town in W---s. He was then in perfect health. One night he retired to rest in peculiarly good spirits, and as his custom was, for it was then summer, he sat near the window and gazed for some time on the beauties of nature.

He then amused himself for a while by humming a tune, when presently on looking towards the door, he saw the figure of a man enter. His dress was a blood-red night cap, flannel jacket, and breeches. The man approached the bed, his countenance and walk indicating extreme illness, threw himself upon it, gave several groans, and apparently expired.

My friend was so filled with horror that he lost all power of speech and motion, and remained fixed on his seat 'til morning, when he told his landlord the occurrence of the night, and declared that unless they could find him other apartments he would leave them that very day. The honest people were disinclined to part with him and agreed to accommodate him on the ground floor. About twelve months after this, he went out on a market day for the purpose of purchasing some provisions, and when he returned, he heard that his old room was taken, but what was his surprise to find in the new lodger the very form, with the very same dress that had so terrified him a year before!

The man was then very ill. He died in a few weeks, and the circumstances were without any exception the same as those which my friend had witnessed. This is one of those cases in which it is extremely difficult to ascertain the design of the appearance.

I should much like to know what conjecture you would form, as to the *modus* and end of such a singular incident.

Of the veracity of the narrator it was impossible for me to doubt. As this minister is still living, I am not at liberty to mention his name.

Pray excuse the freedom of thus addressing you, and believe me to be, Madam, with every sentiment of respect and esteem,

Yours, very truly, Mrs. C. Crowe,

R. I. O.

Letter 3

Gloucestershire, June 21, 1854
MADAM,

As I find that another communication will not be unacceptable, I proceed to detail a few cases. My first relates to the minister, a part of whose history I have given you, and belongs to the class of prophetic dreams. When he had resolved to study for the ministry and through the influence of friends, he had obtained admission to a Dissenting College.[78] As the day affixed for his departure drew near, he was filled with anxiety, from the fact that he had not even money to pay his traveling expenses.

He did not like to borrow, and he had no reason to conclude that anyone suspected the miserable state of his finances. The evening before his expected removal, he lay down to rest with a troubled heart. This was in the very same seaport where the circumstance happened which I have already told you. After some hours of great mental suffering, sleep came to his relief, and in his dream there seemed to approach him one of a most pleasing form, who told him that he not only saw that he was in distress, but that he well knew the cause of it, and that if he would walk down on the beach to a certain place which he pointed out as in a picture, he would find under some loose stones enough for his present necessities.

In the morning, accordingly, almost as soon as it was light he hastened to the indicated spot, and to his great surprise and delight found a sum amounting to a trifle more than was absolutely necessary

---

[78] British educational entities run on "nonconformist" principles in relation to the Church of England.

for his journey. I would just, in passing, remark that he said that on another occasion, his father who died many years before appeared to him with an angry countenance, and assured him that he would suffer much from something he had done in reference to his family, but as this was evidently an unpleasant and even painful topic I did not wish him to enlarge upon it.

The other fact I shall mention happened to my grandfather, who was also a minister. I am well aware that it is of such a nature that the relation of it would in most companies excite a burst of laughter or at least a contemptuous and skeptical smile, but I know I am addressing one who has studied in a very different school of philosophy.

It was in the large town of B---m where my grandfather resided for many years, that the event took place. He himself my grandfather, my aunts, and my mother used often to tell it to their friends when the conversation turned on the supernatural. I have probably heard it a hundred times and I am not ashamed to say that on the testimony of such a man as my grandfather I cannot but yield to it my belief.

One morning when breakfast had just commenced, my grandfather went from the table, at which my grandmother also was sitting, into the passage, for what purpose I have now forgotten, and there he found, for the front door had been standing open, a strange-looking man in black, with a shuffling gait and a club foot. He declared that he had an instantaneous conviction that this was a supernatural appearance, and that a spirit of evil stood before him.

The man in black exclaimed, moving towards the breakfast room, "I am come to take breakfast with you this morning."

My grandfather, convulsively seizing the handle of the door, said, with a stern look, "You are too late, sir," to which the other instantly replied, "I am not too late for the remnant," and then rushed into the street.

My grandfather followed, and to his amazement saw this creature at the top of the street, which was of great length, and in a moment or two he vanished. My grandmother heard a loud talking, and when my grandfather returned to the table in considerable agitation, she naturally wished to know what had occurred, but as she was near her confinement he of course concealed the matter from her. The mysterious words of the stranger followed him continually, and he puzzled himself in seeking to explain their meaning. In a few days my grandmother was confined. The child was dead-born and her life for some time hung in jeopardy. He now believed he had arrived at the solution of the difficulty: the infant was the "remnant" referred to.

I am not the subject of remarkable dreams. I had one, however, lately, and I give it you because it stands connected in my mind with the knowledge of a singular psychical fact which I am confident will greatly interest you, if you have not yet fallen upon it in the course of your reading.

About a fortnight ago, I thought I saw in my sleep a young man, who is assistant to our principal surgeon, come into my room, looking exceedingly unwell. He laid himself on the other bed in my chamber, and I thought that he had come there to linger out his last illness, at which I felt not the least surprise or objection. He seemed to be perfectly resigned, and presently he began to converse with me, and after we had talked for some time, whilst he was replying to something I had said, I distinctly saw his spirit rise up out of his body.

He gazed at the corpse with the deepest interest and pleasure. One moment he would stand by the head and survey the face, and the next move to the feet, and then gaze at the entire body. He called me to come and stand by his side and view this lifeless frame, which I did with as much placidity as he seemed himself to possess, and without the slightest idea of their being anything absurd in what I saw.

I could not, however, help saying "O, that I could leave my body and have such a view of it as you have now of yours!"

I remember no more. In the morning I had occasion to call on a friend, who has a large library containing many rare books. Not being in the humor for close reading, for I spend many hours at a time there, I took up from a center table a volume of a lighter kind. It happened to be Mrs. Child's *Letters from New York*.[79]

Turning the leaves over carelessly, my eye lighted on a chapter headed "The spirit surveying its own body!" She there says that she was told by a pious lady, that when once in a swoon, she felt that she left the body and was standing by it during the whole time it lasted, that she distinctly heard every word spoken by the doctor and her family, and saw every movement of their countenances, and all that was done with her body. I may observe that I have not heard that anything has occurred to the young man I saw. If I have not already tired your patience you may draw on my memory for something more. A line to that effect will oblige,

Yours very truly, Mrs. Crowe,

R. I. O.

---

[79] Lydia Maria Francis Child (1802 - 1880) was an American writer and political activist. *Letters* was a regular column in an abolitionist newspaper, collected into a book in 1843. This incident, "The Soul watching its own Body," appears in Letter XIX.

Edinburgh, August 10th
MADAM,

In consequence of a long absence abroad, I never had, 'til recently, an opportunity of reading your agreeable work, *The Night Side of Nature*, which contains a mass of evidence in favor of your theories, to which I take the liberty of adding a few cases from my own experience.

Many years ago I lived in a house in Edinburgh, which belonged to my mother's relatives, and in which my maternal grandfather had died, several years antecedent to my own birth. The room in which I slept was that, but at the time unknown to me, in which my relative had expired.

There were two beds in the room, one a large four-poster and the other a sort of couch. The latter was next the door, and both lay between it and the window, which was barred and bolted, and opposite to them was the fireplace, with rather a high mantelpiece. Being summer, the "board" was on the chimney.

It was about eleven o'clock at night; the rest of the family had retired to rest. As there were only about two inches of candle left, I placed the candlestick on the mantelpiece, intending to allow it to burn out, and went to my bed, which was on the couch. I had just lay down, and was looking towards the candle, when, to my extreme horror, I perceived a tall old man in his nightdress, standing by the mantelpiece.

His sight seemed impaired, for he put forth his hand and felt for something, and then moved across the fireplace, in doing which, he obscured the light on passing it. My gaze was riveted on him. He then turned towards the large bed on my left, and stretching out his hands attempted with a feeble effort to lay himself down, and in doing so I heard him sigh distinctly.

He disappeared almost at the same moment. He did not appear to have noticed me. I immediately sprang out of bed and opening the door on my right hand, called out loudly, but never left the doorway, as I was resolved that if the figure were that of a living person there should be no means of egress. On the assembling of the family in my room, a search was made, but there was nothing to be seen, and there had been no possibility of a human being having been in the room.

The affair was put down to an illusion. Yet so strong an impression did it leave on my mind, that a few years since (1851 or '52), when in

India, I published in Saunder's Magazine,[80] printed at the Delhi Gazette press, an account of this apparition, in a narrative, which I wrote called "Idone, or Incidents in the life of a dreamer,"[81] and which with the exception of this introductory vision, was, in reality, a series of actual dreams of which I had kept a record, and this I endeavored to weave into a vague story, with the view of illustrating how a person might live two distinct lives!

Sometime after the above were published, I read with much interest, *Swedenborg's Theory of the Spiritual World*,[82] and lately when reading your work, I was struck with some peculiar resemblances between my own experience and the cases you cite.

But to return to the family and house in Edinburgh, of my grandfather. Other members of the family have seen unaccountable figures in the same house. An aunt of mine and a cousin, one night, met an old woman on the stairs with a large bunch of keys, and were in the greatest alarm. On another occasion, on going to open a room which had been locked up for some time, in order to prepare it for the reception of my eldest uncle, who had just returned that night from abroad, two members of the family started back and locked the door again, for on entering they had both seen the mattress and etc. violently heaved up. On returning with the servants, nothing was visible of an unusual description.

Again, two relatives occupied the same room, and one night, as the fire was burning low, after they had gone to bed, the door being locked, they were alarmed by a sound like wings, over their beds, and by a dusky form moving about the room. It walked up to the fireplace and seemed restless. When it had disappeared, they both rose and unlocked the door, called for assistance, but, as usual, nothing of their visitor was to be seen.

A still more remarkable incident occurred in the same house. As two of my aunts were sitting opposite the window, at night, they were startled by the apparition of an absent brother-in-law looking in, and with a pen in his hand. A few days afterwards the intelligence of his death arrived. He had been signing his will at the exact time they had seen his apparition.

---

[80] According to the *Images of India* website, *Saunders' Monthly Magazine* was published from 1851-1854, and printed at the Delhi Gazette Press by Kunniah Lall.

[81] This identifies the writer of the letter as J.H.L. (James Henry Lawrence) Archer.

[82] Emanuel Swedenborg (1688 – 1772) was a scientist turned mystic whose works famously influenced William Blake, among others. He was a prolific writer, but this does not appear to be the English-language title of a specific book, though it may have been an excerpt or popular translation.

My eldest uncle, shortly after his return from abroad, went to Musselburgh[83] to visit an old schoolmaster, and as he entered the yard he observed him limping into the school. He tried to overtake him, and on reaching the door he met one of the tutors, who informed him that the doctor had been confined to his bed for some time with a broken leg.

The same uncle, who was an officer in the army, dreamt that he had obtained his captaincy by the retirement of an officer of the name of Patterson (so far as I remember). There was no such officer then in the regiment, and he mentioned it as strange that he should have dreamt of a particular name. A few Gazettes[84] afterwards, my uncle obtained his promotion by an officer of this name being brought in from the half-pay to sell out in the same Gazette.

I have myself heard the most remarkable and unaccountable noises in my grandfather's house. The servants were often in the greatest terror. I have heard, seemingly, the whole of the furniture, in a particular room, thrown violently about, accompanied with the noise of something rolling on the floor. At other times I have distinctly heard, as it were, a boy's marble falling step by step down the stairs and striking against my door, which was at the foot of them, and yet this was at night, and there were no children in the house. This annoyance, with that of steps heard round my bed, was so common as to cease to make any impression on me.

I may mention that my grandfather was not happy in his family relations, and died in an uneasy frame of mind, on Christmas Eve, 1820. Since my family sold his house, I have never heard that its new occupants were disturbed.

I have at different periods of my life had groups, as it were, of very remarkable allegorical dreams.

It is somewhat singular that involuntary efforts may be made during sleep, which are I believe beyond the bounds of possibility during waking moments. Indeed, the curious phenomena which you have so ably criticized, are without limit.

Though you do not approve of the concealment of names, I hope you will excuse my asking you to do so in the present instance as many of the parties concerned might be displeased.

I have the honor to remain, Madam, Your obedient servant,

Anonymous

---

[83] A Scottish town six miles from Edinburgh.
[84] An announcement in an official publication.

P.S. I know two remarkable instances of prophetic denunciation[85] or the power of will, under, of course, the control of Providence. In one instance, the death of the party denounced followed on the week predicted, although at the time he was well. Moreover, the denunciation was never mentioned to him.

In the other instance, the accomplishment of the denunciation was accomplished to the exact day, and under very remarkable circumstances. I believe this power to be involuntary, and more of the nature of inspiration.

Happy Holidays from the Skull and Book Press!

---

[85] The use of religions prophecy for condemnation.